BOBBY LEE CLAREMONT

AND THE

CRIMINAL ELEMENT

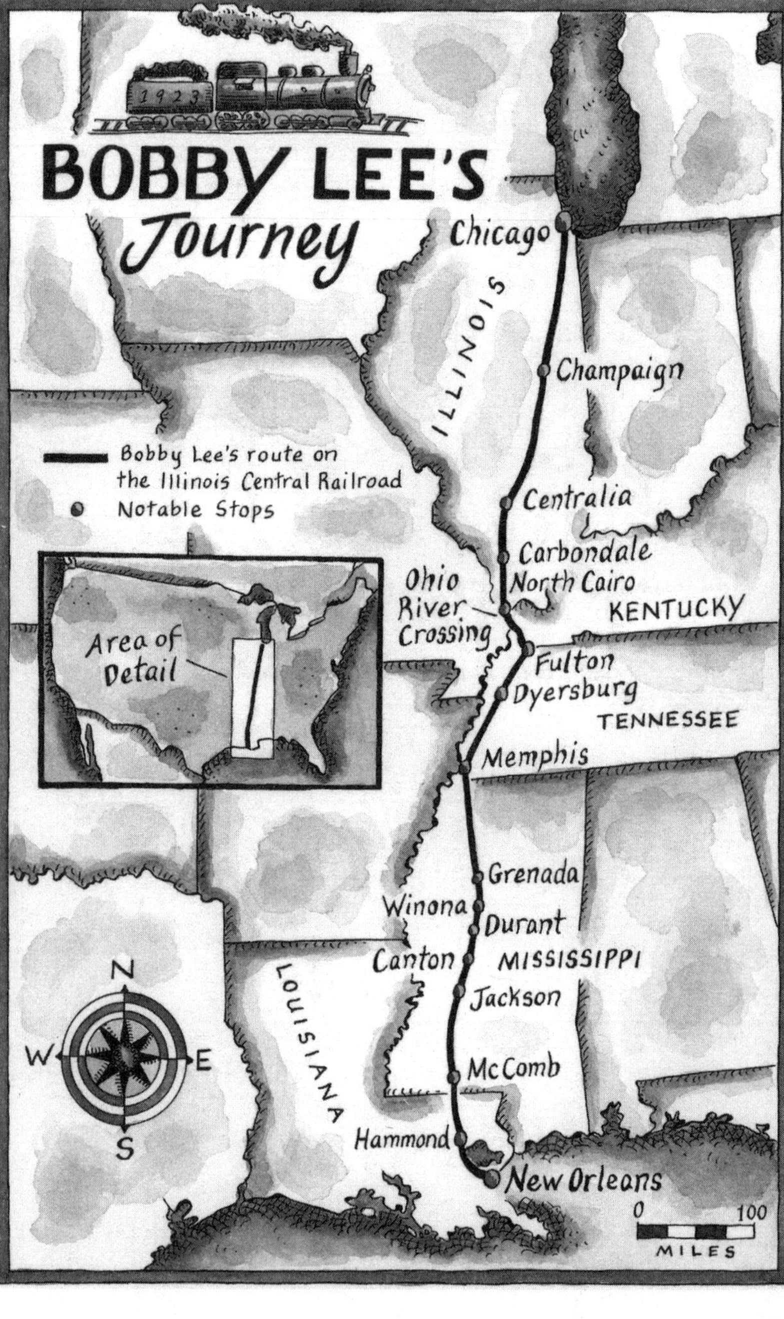
1923
BOBBY LEE'S
Journey
Chicago
ILLINOIS
Champaign
Bobby Lee's route on
the Illinois Central Railroad
Notable Stops
Centralia
Carbondale
North Cairo
Ohio
River
Crossing
KENTUCKY
Area of
Detail
Fulton
Dyersburg
TENNESSEE
Memphis
Grenada
Winona
Durant
Canton
MISSISSIPPI
LOUISIANA
Jackson
N
W
E
S
McComb
Hammond
New Orleans
0
100
MILES

BOBBY LEE CLAREMONT AND THE CRIMINAL ELEMENT

Jeannie Mobley

Holiday House / New York

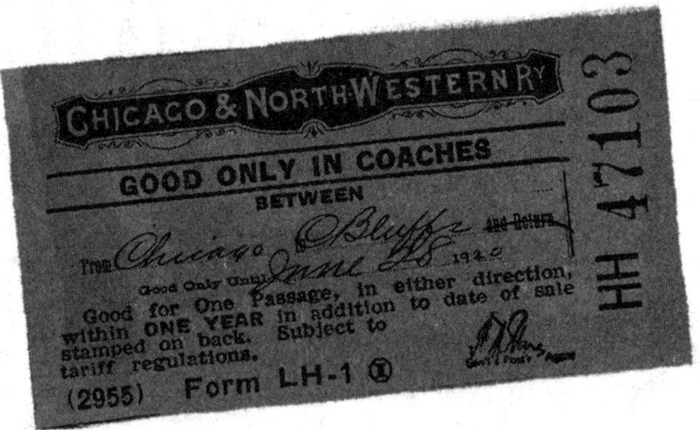

Printed and bound in August 2017 at Maple Press, York, PA, USA.
www.holidayhouse.com
First Edition

1 3 5 7 9 10 8 6 4 2

Library of Congress Cataloging-in-Publication Data

Names: Mobley, Jeannie, author.
Title: Bobby Lee Claremont and the criminal element / Jeannie Mobley.
Description: First edition. | New York : Holiday House, [2017] | Summary: In 1923, when New Orleans native and orphan Bobby Lee Claremont boards a train to Chicago, where he hopes to join the criminal element and make a new life for himself, far away from the heavy-handed salvation of the Sisters of Charitable Mercy, he acquaints himself with a group of intriguing and possibly dangerous passengers who cause Bobby Lee to reconsider his plans.
Identifiers: LCCN 2016051682 | ISBN 9780823437818 (hardcover)
Subjects: | CYAC: Railroad trains—Fiction. | Runaways—Fiction. | Orphans—Fiction. | Criminals—Fiction. | Mystery and detective stories.
Classification: LCC PZ7.M71275 Bo 2017 | DDC [Fic]—dc23 LC record available at https://lccn.loc.gov/2016051682

for Greg—my pride, my joy, my own little
criminal element all grown up.
I love you, man.

MAY 27, 1923
NEW ORLEANS, LOUISIANA
7:45 A.M.

I shifted my weight from one foot to the other and glanced at the huge clock on the wall. According to the timetable below it, the train to Chicago—and freedom—would pull out of the station in fifteen minutes, whether I was on it or not. But that didn't make one measly bit of difference to the lady ahead of me at the ticket counter, who was rooting around in the bottom of her pocketbook for the remainder of her fare. The minute hand on the clock eased forward a tick as she picked out one penny after another, like she had all the time in the world. All the time and none of the sense, far as I could tell.

Imagine losing track of money! I'd made plenty of mistakes in my life, but that sure wasn't one of them. I knew where every last cent of mine was: safe and sound inside my pocket. Excepting, of course, the two pennies I had placed on Maman's eyes when we laid her in the crypt. I could still see that bright copper against her alabaster face. It had been hard to give up two cents, but then again I figured I owed her that much, what with all I had cost her. Two pennies didn't make much difference to getting me out of New Orleans. And I *had* to get out of New Orleans.

That's why I'd turned to the poor box of the Sisters of Charitable Mercy. I knew it was a sin to steal—lord knows, Sister Mary Magdalene had drummed that into my head often enough—but the box had barely even been locked. And anyway, I reckoned it was a solid start on my new life of crime, which was about all I was good for. Thirteen years old, and I had already lied, cheated, and killed my mother, more or less. Stealing from a church was a nice addition to my résumé, seeing as how I was headed to Chicago to set myself up in a life of crime for good. Or at least I would be setting off, if the lady at the counter would get moving. If I could get my ticket and get on that train before either the Sisters or the police found the empty poor box and tracked me down.

At last, with a strange little "Ooh!" of satisfaction, the woman found her last penny, laid it on the counter, and scooted it under the barrier to the ticket master. He counted her money with painful deliberateness before sliding a ticket back to her. She snapped her pocketbook shut, straightened her hair and hat with one lace-gloved hand, picked up her ticket, picked up her carpetbag, double-checked the counter just in case she had forgotten any change, looked at the board to find her platform, and *finally* stepped out of the way.

I pressed forward to the counter and looked the ticket master square in the eyes, as if buying a train ticket to Chicago was old hat to me. Folks like me, aiming for a life of crime, know that confidence is the key to deception. Confidence, though, wasn't enough to hide the fact that I was only thirteen—and a small thirteen at that, since the Sisters of Charitable Mercy hadn't been nearly as charitable as I would have liked when it came to their free lunches. The closest I'd ever been to satisfied was that narrow space between not quite hungry and not quite full. Now, as the ticket master looked down at me, his blue eyes in their own narrow space between bushy eyebrows and half-moon spectacles, he wasn't all that satisfied neither. He watched me unfold the scrap of newspaper from my pocket and remove from it miscellaneous coins until I had the exact fare laid out on the counter.

"You traveling to Chicago all by yourself?" he said doubtfully.

"Yes, sir. I got me a Yankee aunt up there," I lied. Another sin piled onto my morning's tally, but after a lifetime of sinning, topped off by robbing the poor box in a church, I figured God would hardly even notice. Plus, I needed the practice if I was going to be a criminal. I had to get to where my conscience hardly even noticed either, which wasn't going to be easy after all the hours I'd spent in the company of Sister Mary Magdalene and all her long-winded charitable mercy. I'd done plenty of lying, cheating, and stealing for as long as I could remember, but I'd done plenty of penance too.

"What about your momma and daddy?" asked the ticket master. "Ain't they here to see you off?"

"Yes, sir, that's my daddy over yonder," I said, pointing to a stranger standing by himself near the door. This time, it might not have been a lie. Maman had never told me who my daddy was; maybe she hadn't known herself. In my case, it seemed even being born had been a sin.

"He wants me to buy my own ticket, to prove I'm old enough to travel alone. My aunt will meet me at the station in Chicago."

I smiled and looked the ticket master in the eye again, willing him to hurry. Only six minutes until the train pulled out.

The ticket master scrutinized the stranger I'd pointed out, and his eyebrows gradually slid back down to where they belonged. He counted out the money I'd put on the counter with slow hands, moving like a winding-down clock. It was my time that was running out—in more ways than one. When I had pointed out my "daddy" to the ticket master, I had noticed new arrivals entering the station. Four policemen in uniform, and I recognized one of them. He had helped return runaway orphans to the Sisters of Charitable Mercy so often that Sister Mary Magdalene called him by his Christian name. They had found the empty poor box. I had to get on that train before it left, and before they spotted me.

I nudged my hat down a little lower over my face and turned back to the ticket counter. The ticket master had pulled the ticket and was saying something about baggage. I interrupted him.

"Which platform?"

"Two. That way. Better get on over there, it departs soon."

He didn't have to tell me twice, not with those cops starting to spread out through the station. I turned toward the entryways to the platforms and set off at a trot.

Other late passengers were hurrying toward their destinations as well, and I slipped into the thick, rushing crowd, trying to disappear. When I was at last in the shadowed archway I broke into a run, bursting out onto the platform. I crashed head-on into a group of burly workmen. One of them cursed and nearly dropped his end of their heavy load. I stumbled backward and fell, landing square on my backside.

I looked up. A shock ran through me when I saw what the workmen were carrying—a long pine box, like the one Maman had been closed in just a week ago. As I sat, stunned, the four men heaved the coffin up to the edge of an open baggage car on the train. *My* train—bound for Chicago.

The crowds of late folks kept surging past, cursing as they swerved or stumbled over me, but I couldn't move. I sat transfixed, watching the workmen slide that coffin into the car, seeing again my mother's coffin sliding into the dark maw of the Sisters' crypt for the poor. Sister Bernadette had offered me her hand then. Now, it was a kid about my own age who offered to help me up. The hand he extended was friendly enough, and I took hold of it, realizing as I did that it was rough and callused from hard work—and much darker than my own. I looked around, embarrassed to find myself in a crowd of colored folk, all hugging and saying goodbye to family as they boarded the car reserved for them, right behind the baggage car.

I looked again at the boy who'd helped me. He was looking at me, just as curious. He wore denim overalls, with no shirt underneath, and his dark arms and chest were moist with sweat. Judging from the two large suitcases on either side of him, he'd probably been loading the baggage car before I'd come crashing through, though he wasn't any older than me. As soon as I let go his hand, he tucked it, along with the other, into the bib of the overalls. A younger boy stood at his elbow, a skinny kid of about five or six, in a shirt and trousers several sizes too big for him. When I looked at him, he stuffed his hands into his pants pockets, and grinned. His teeth were crooked, and the front two were missing, but he didn't seem to mind showing them off in a friendly smile.

"I don't think you're in the right place," said the younger boy, lisping a little through his missing front teeth.

"You can say that again," I said, glancing around at all the smiling faces. I didn't belong among so many people feeling happy and warm in the comfort of family, no matter what color my skin was. I glanced again at the baggage car, and the coffin, which I could still see through the open door.

"There's a dead man in that box," the younger boy said, following my gaze. "And we aim to find out who it is."

"Hush up, Terrance," the older boy said.

"It's true," said the younger boy. "And there's a lady in widow's weeds who got on the train. We reckon she's mournin' whoever's in that box—"

"Hush *up*," the older boy repeated before turning back to me. "Where you headed?"

"Chicago. To visit my aunt," I added quickly, before they could ask.

"You got a Yankee aunt?" Terrance asked in a surprised tone. I couldn't tell whether he was impressed or suspicious.

"Mind your own business, Terrance," the older boy said before turning back to me. "I meant, can I help you find your car?"

"Do you work here?" I asked.

The younger boy giggled, but the older one elbowed him.

"Why else would I be hauling these suitcases? I ain't stealing them, if that's what you think," he said, a little defensively.

"I didn't say you were," I said, thinking as I did it would be a good scam, and one I might remember in case I needed a little cash once I got to Chicago.

"Let me see your ticket," he said.

I held it out to him and he pointed farther along the train, to where the cars looked newer and nicer. "Car number 4, right there. Best be getting aboard. She'll be pulling out directly."

"Maybe we'll see you on down the line," the younger boy called after me as I hurried to my coach. I didn't answer. I had recovered from the shock of seeing the coffin enough to remember the police, and I was eager to board and get out of sight before they found me.

Still, I couldn't quite shake the heebie-jeebies that had come over me. I reckoned that was another thing I'd have to get over in a life of crime, but I couldn't help feeling like it was all part of my punishment from God. Far as I could tell, me and God had never been on particularly good terms, but I figured he was spitting mad now, what with me robbing a church and all. Putting that coffin in my path had been his little way of reminding me that he'd be serving up some just desserts for my sins, and they wouldn't be pralines or bread pudding, neither.

I mounted the steps and entered the coach from the first door I came to at the front. It was the cheapest whites-only car on the train, not a Pullman sleeper where I could rest in comfort on the twenty-three-hour trip, but a coach car, where any sleeping to be done would be on the stiff wooden benches. I slipped into an empty seat near the back, swinging my small bag off my shoulder, and hunched down low so I couldn't be seen through the window. The last of the passengers scurried aboard and the doors closed. Bystanders on the platform began waving hands and handkerchiefs as the brakes let out in a huge, steamy belch. The engine huffed and the train cars lurched and strained against the couplings before easing forward.

Out on the platform a policeman appeared, but if he was out to catch me he was too late. The platform was already sliding away behind us. I smiled to myself and sat up straight. I had escaped—escaped from the cops and the constant reminders of Maman's ruination and death in New Orleans.

I pulled the bit of newspaper, now empty of its coins, from my pocket and smoothed it across my knee. The headline blazed large and bold: MORE LIQUOR PRODUCED IN CHICAGO THAN BEFORE PROHIBITION. I read the next sentence too, about criminals making millions of dollars and dining with the mayor. That's the one I liked, the one that held all the promise. I figured a sweet-faced sinner like me could make a decent living in the town where men like Johnny Torrio and Al Capone ran the show. Sure, I'd have to spend a little time on the streets, maybe run a rigged shell game or two, maybe charm a few meals out of little old ladies who couldn't resist a motherless boy with such good manners. But I'd find a way to catch a bootlegger's eye somehow. That was the thing about scraping by—you learned to keep one eye always open for opportunity. And when it came knocking, I would throw the door wide open and let it sweep me away to easy street.

I folded the newspaper carefully and slipped it back into my pocket, glancing around at the other passengers, feeling smug in my recent escape and bright future. Other than the porter in his alcove near the door, the coach car was nearly empty. There was only one small party of travelers at the rear of the car and a single man off to my right. I guess most folks paid the extra for a bed for the night in a Pullman sleeper.

The lone man to my right wore a rumpled brown suit and was reading a newspaper. The party at the other end consisted of three men and a lady. One man was slender, and pale, like he'd never been out in the sun. The other two were big and bigger, making the lady between them seem as tiny and frail as a sparrow. As for her, even though she was facing toward me, I could not see her face. She was dressed head to toe in widow's weeds—black hat, black veil, black dress. Against her shoulder, like an angelic cloud of innocence amid the trappings of her grief, slept a tiny baby, wrapped in a soft, white cotton blanket, its head tucked up all peaceful on her shoulder.

I thought again of the coffin in the baggage car, my heart sinking as I realized it held a husband and father. This was a woman and a baby cast adrift in the cruel world. Despite my vow to become a hardened criminal, I hated the sight of that fatherless child. It was as if I was seeing me and Maman, back in the beginning, back before she had worked herself to death for my sake. Maybe I'd once been innocent like that too, before life had gobbled us up and spit us out onto the streets, where swiping rolls from bakeries and loose change from pockets had been the best way to survive. Maybe Maman had once held me like that, long before holding on to me had killed her.

I blinked and forced my vision of the widow and baby to come back into focus. Innocence was for saps and patsies,

I told myself. I was headed to Chicago to make my mark on the underworld. Fame, fortune, and a life of leisure—that's what I was after, and none of those came with good, honest hard work. My dead, hardworking Maman was proof enough of that.

HAMMOND, LOUISIANA
9:45 A.M.

New Orleans disappeared behind us and the train picked up speed through the bayous, rocking into a steady rhythm, the rails clattering beneath us in a metallic beat. Inside the carriage, everything was quiet. The man in the brown suit read his paper. The rest of us just sat. I looked out the window, watched the trees and moss and mud, the green and wild world so different from the city streets that had raised me. A little thrill ran through me—I had truly left home now.

The train rolled on and the bayous flashed by for forty-five minutes. Then the conductor walked through the car to announce our first stop, at Hammond, Louisiana. As if the train had heard him, the rhythm shifted and the wheels began to slow. At last, with a shriek and huff of the brakes, we stopped amid a cluster of little houses. Only the presence of the ramshackle, single-room depot gave the place the nerve to call itself a town.

The only thing coming or going from Hammond, Louisiana, was the mail. Out my window, I caught sight of the colored boy in the overalls hauling the mail sacks to the baggage car and hoisting them up to a man inside. It struck me as strange. All the other workers I'd seen were grown men. Maybe this boy had lied about his age to get a job, as I had once done at the docks of the United Fruit Company. That had been a good, honest job—except, of course, for the lying I'd had to do to get it. It hadn't paid much, barely enough to keep a roof over our heads when Maman had grown too sick to work. Then Sister Mary Magdalene had found out and gone to my bosses with the truth about my age. I was out of a job, and back in the convent's poorhouse, while Maman was sent to their hospital. I suppose for Sister Mary Magdalene that was a charitable mercy, but not for me.

While the boy loaded the mail, two little colored girls came onto the train with baskets full of homemade pralines, roasted peanuts, and warm corn pones for sale. My mouth watered as my fellow travelers made their purchases, but I only had two cents left after paying my fare to Chicago. It might buy an apple or a handful of peanuts somewhere along the way, but I figured it was safer to hold on to it, just in case.

I turned my thoughts back to my days on the docks, trying to ignore the hot, oily aroma of nuts and fresh-fried corn bread. The dock was where I had seen my first Yankee gangster, first realized how high on the hog a man could live with a good, dishonest job. Because while I had been sweating and straining to earn my pennies, I'd watched the fellow disembark from a gilded riverboat, as lazy and smug as a cat in the sun. A swaggering, pin-striped, polished peacock of a white man, his watch chain glinting in the sunlight across his well-fed belly. The beautiful blond woman on his arm was all but swallowed up by long strands of expensive pearls, bright rouge coloring her lily-white cheeks. And as they walked, she kept glancing at him from under her lashes, like he was more than just the bees knees—he was the whole sweet hive, dripping with honey.

"Who's that?" I'd asked the fellow working next to me.

"That's trouble," the fellow said.

"What kind of trouble?" I asked, thinking that I sure wouldn't mind being in that kind of trouble.

"The kind from up north, kid. The kind that will cut off your nose just for staring at him. So forget about him and get back to work."

I got back to work, but I didn't forget about him. And the more I thought about him, the more sure I was that he was a gangster—maybe Johnny Torrio himself—living large and easy. All the money and food and comfort a body could ask for. Soft hands and clean fingernails and meat with every meal. No toiling like I'd been doing on the dock.

Or for that matter, I now thought as I looked out the train window, toiling like the older boy on the station platform. As I watched him hoisting the last of the canvas mailbags on board, I reached into my pocket and felt for the newspaper clipping.

"More liquor produced in Chicago than before Prohibition," I whispered. When I saw the headline only a day after Maman's funeral, I remembered the dapper Yankee from the docks. I took it for a sign that it was time to start a new life in Chicago.

The final mailbag disappeared into the baggage car and the boy jumped up after it. A moment later, the workmen on the platform slid the door of the compartment shut. This piqued my curiosity. How would the boy get back out of the baggage car? Before I could contemplate the answer, a voice cut into my thoughts.

"Would you like a corn pone, son? Allow me."

I nearly jumped out of my skin. The man in the brown suit who had been reading the paper was now standing in the aisle beside me, grinning down at me. He waved over one of the girls and took five corn pones from her basket, piling them on a clean handkerchief in his hand. When he had all he wanted, he reached into his pocket, smearing its edge with grease, and pulled out a nickel for the girl. Then he shooed her away with a flick of his hand, as if she was no more than a pigeon in the street. She scuttled away, head down, trying to be invisible as she retreated from the train car. I frowned. Working the docks and the streets, I'd learned that the colored folks were just trying to get by like the rest of us. The way he got what he wanted and then scorned her told me all I needed to know about this man. But he dismissed my frown as well, and settled himself uninvited into the seat opposite me. He held out the pile of corn pones on the handkerchief.

"Eat 'em while they're warm. Go on, son."

"Thank you, sir," I said. I wanted to tell him I wasn't his son, but instead I just helped myself to the biggest corn pone and prepared for whatever was coming. I'd lived off charity often enough to know that people didn't buy you breakfast without expecting something in return. Sure enough, after I'd swallowed the last bite and licked the grease from my fingers he smiled at me, as if to say he had me in his debt and planned to make the most of it.

"What's your name, son?" he said in that easy, friendly voice untrustworthy folks use when they want you to trust them. I didn't, but since he still had a handful of golden corn bread, and I still had an empty stomach, I smiled back.

"Robert E. Lee Claremont, sir," I said, trying to give off a whiff of innocence.

He gave a whistle of appreciation. "That's a mighty fine name, son. A mighty fine name. Have another."

He held out the handkerchief again and I took another corn pone. This was exactly why Maman had given me the name, and why I had shared it with him. A boy needed every advantage he could get in this hard world, she always said. For a while I couldn't see how being named after the South's greatest failure was an advantage, but with uppity white men in New Orleans it often paid off.

"Thank you, sir," I said again. "And what's your name?"

He smiled as polite as could be. "I'm Sergeant Rufus T. Hayworth, and pleased to be makin' your acquaintance."

I froze, the corn bread halfway to my mouth. Sergeant? The train lurched and began moving again.

"Are you a soldier, sir?" I asked, hoping against hope.

He chuckled and pulled back his jacket to reveal the badge on his sweat-stained shirt. "I'm a member of the Louisiana State Police, son. And I was just wondering what a youngster your age was doing, traveling alone on such a long journey. You're headed to Chicago, I presume?"

"Call me Bobby Lee," I said. If he was fixin' to drag me back to the Sisters of Charitable Mercy, he might as well call me by my sinner's name. I was only Robert when Sister Mary

Magdalene was making me walk the straight and narrow. "I'm going to visit my aunt. She'll be meeting me at the station in Chicago."

"That so?" said the sergeant, his tone still friendly and conversational, though his eyes were telling me he didn't believe me. "What's this aunt's name?"

"Aunt Bertha, sir," I said quickly, knowing hesitation could give away a liar, then wondering if I'd given it away by being too quick. "She's got a fine, big car. She's meeting me at the station." I swallowed to make myself shush up before I got in any deeper.

Maybe I was too deep already. Sergeant Hayworth was looking at me in that long, hard, considering way, and I couldn't tell where he'd end up after all that considering.

"The thing is," he said after a spell, "I couldn't help noticing the way you hunkered down in your seat before we left New Orleans, like you didn't want to be seen through the windows. Like maybe someone might be looking for you."

He paused, waited for me to crack. I blinked and chewed, and waited right back, giving away nothing.

He frowned, flattening his eyebrows down tight so that his eyes went all hard. "The thing is," he said again, leaning in this time, like he was sharing a secret, "I have it on good authority that those folks behind me, at the rear of the car, they aren't respectable, if you take my meaning. Could be mighty dangerous for a boy on his own. Mighty dangerous."

I leaned to look around him at the woman and three men, who seemed to be minding their business. My heart gave a little flutter of hope. "You mean they're criminals?"

"They might be, son. They very well might be."

"What kind of criminals?" I asked, trying not to let my rising excitement show.

"Murderers," he whispered, in a way meant to scare me. "Cold-blooded killers, son."

I leaned out for another quick peek before bending closer and whispering, "Even the baby?"

"Of course not the baby! But the others, they could be unpredictable, and mighty dangerous. So maybe you might want to tell me your real story, son? Where you belong?"

I looked him square in the eye, steady as could be. "Yes, sir. I belong with my Aunt Bertha in Chicago. She'll be coming for me in her fine, big car, sir."

He leaned back then, disappointed that I hadn't spilled my guts. "'Course you do. But you be careful, you hear? You tell me if them folks try anything suspicious on this journey. I'm a police officer, and I'll protect you as best as I can."

So that was it. He wanted me to be a snitch and thought he'd buy my services with two corn pones and a little fear. I didn't say anything, just gave him a meaningless smile, formulating my own plan.

"Well," the sergeant said, getting to his feet and dusting the crumbs off his jacket. "I think I need a cup o' joe to wash down that corn bread. It's been a pleasure talking to you, Robert E. Lee Claremont."

He walked to the back of the carriage and opened the door. The clack of the wheels on the track filled the air for a brief moment before the door closed behind him. I continued to look straight ahead, with equal parts curiosity and trepidation. With the policeman gone, I had an unencumbered view of the group at the far end of the carriage. Now that he mentioned it, I *could* see the rakish tilt of a hat and the pinstripes on a suit. And was that the glint of a solid gold watch chain?

Criminals! Exactly who I wanted to meet! Only problem was, the big man sitting beside the widow had been watching me the whole time I'd been conversing with Sergeant Hayworth. And he looked none too happy that I had been fraternizing with the enemy.

SOMEWHERE NEAR THE MISSISSIPPI STATE LINE 9:55 A.M.

I slid across the seat to the wall and looked out the window. The swamps with their curtains of drooping moss were giving way to farmland as we neared the state line. Louisiana was almost behind me for good. I chewed my lip and planned my next move. I had to play it cool. If these folks were criminals, they were exactly the type I wanted to impress. Not that I wanted to fall in with a gang of murderers, but Hayworth could have just made that up to scare me. Besides, these people were clean, well dressed. They looked respectable, in the way that only money and comfortable living could make a person respectable, and that was the kind of respectable I wanted to be. After all, if my criminal ambitions only extended as far as pocket picking and back-alley thuggery, I could have stayed in New Orleans. I was headed to Chicago, where, according to the papers, the crooks walked the streets in three-piece suits and dined with the mayor. *That* was the kind of criminal element I belonged with, and if this was my first encounter with them, I didn't want to look like a rube straight off the bayous.

Of course, I would have to tread carefully with a cop in the car. I wished I hadn't told Sergeant Hayworth my real name.

That was hardly a way to impress members of the underworld. If that was, in fact, what they were. Maybe the smell of those corn pones had addled my brain.

After eating just two of them, my mouth was starting to feel more parched than the great Sahara, so I headed for the lavatory at the rear of the carriage. It was a tiny space, just big enough for a sink and a toilet, which was really more just a hole opening right out over the tracks. At the sink, I pumped a little water into my cupped hand and drank. It tasted stale and coppery, but it would do. I pumped and sipped several more times until my thirst was sated. Then I gave myself a good hard look in the mirror. There was nothing I could do to cover the fact that I was poor—the fit of my threadbare clothes and my untrimmed, untidy hair made that obvious—but at least I wanted to make sure my face was clean and I didn't have anything caught between my teeth. I wet my hands one more time and used them to slick down my hair a little, making me look like I'd used a good hair tonic. For a few minutes, anyway, until it dried and fell back over my face.

"How do you do," I said to my reflection. "The name's Bobby Lee Claremont, and if there's something I can do for you—something quick, neat, and discreet—I'm your man." I gave my reflection a sly smile. The reflection smiled back, not really a man yet, but getting there. A few more years and I could start growing a mustache, maybe. Then folks would take me more seriously. Still, there were advantages to my smooth, still-round cheeks, pink and freckled from the sun. I rearranged my smile into that of a cherub, all sweet, youthful innocence, and tousled my hair so that the wet strands curled around my forehead. It was a look that had served me plenty of times. Combined with a tragic fib or two, it could get me a couple of nickels from warmhearted ladies, or sometimes a warm roll or a few beignets for breakfast. The only person who had ever been completely immune to that look was Sister Mary Magdalene, but then again she was a nun. You couldn't expect a nun to have a heart.

I was still studying my face in the mirror, trying to decide on the best look for approaching gangsters, and wondering how I would do it without the cop noticing, when I heard a noise outside the lavatory door. It was a sound I'd heard plenty of times during my stays with the Sisters of Charitable Mercy. A sound I'd be happy to never hear again, but at the moment, one that might be useful.

I turned the knob and opened the door to see the young widow walking the aisle, bouncing her baby as she did. She was halfway down the aisle, as near to my seat as to her own. The child was screaming, and it had a healthy set of lungs, filling the whole car with its protests. I hurried down the aisle toward her, as if just heading back to my own seat. She had been walking the same way, toward the front of the train, and was almost parallel with my seat when she turned back, only to find me coming up behind her. She started and stepped quickly back to avoid running into me. Her sudden move roused the baby into a new wail of protest.

"Sh-sh-sh," she said, patting its back. She tried to step aside to let me pass, but as she did, her long, black lace veil caught fast on a rough splinter of wood on the edge of a seat. Another perfect opportunity for me—luck was smiling on me at last.

I hurried the few steps forward and, bending close to her, unhooked the lace from the wood. She smelled of lavender soap and Cajun cooking, and the scent made my head go a little dizzy.

"Thank you kindly," she said, her voice smooth and rich. The veil had pulled her hat askew and she was trying to push it back into place, but by now the baby was arching its back and swinging its miniature fists like a little prizefighter. One clenched hand managed to grab her veil and was jerking it to and fro, tousling her hair.

"I'll hold the baby if you like, ma'am, while you fix your hat," I said, reaching for the child. I knew how to hold babies from all the time my mother had left me with the nuns. Sister Mary Magdalene had sent me to help Sister Bernadette in the orphanage nursery whenever I gave her a headache, which was pretty often.

The widow hesitated briefly, but her hat was sliding toward the floor now, so she handed the child over. I laid it facedown along my arm and thumped firmly on the little back with my other hand. It squirmed once, gave a hearty belch, and quieted.

The widow removed her hat and veil, then looked at me in surprise. I looked at her with plenty of surprise of my own. Without her veil, she was much younger than I'd expected. Her hair was a glossy black curtain cut in a smooth bob that framed an angel's face of soft, creamy skin, full, shapely lips, and eyes like pools of midnight. She was so pretty my jaw dropped open, but I quickly remembered myself and clamped it shut.

"Well, I'll be," she said. "Where'd you learn to do that?" She gave me a smile that softened my joints to mush. I had to lean my hip against the seat to steady myself.

I swallowed and untied my tongue the best I could. "From my sister, Bernadette," I managed, and immediately felt a twinge of guilt. I didn't like the idea of lying to someone who looked so much like an angel. Still, it wasn't a bona fide lie. Bernadette was *a* Sister, just not *my* sister.

"Does she have many children, your sister?"

"Yes, ma'am," I said, giving her a sweet smile. I needed to change the subject. "What's the baby's name?"

"Jimmy," she said. Then a shadow of sadness crossed her face as she added, "Junior."

"Mind if I hold him a little longer?" I asked. "I might be able to get him to sleep for you. I just love babies."

"That would be mighty fine," she said, and with another smile at me, she sat down in the seat opposite my own. I stayed standing in the aisle as the baby grew limp and heavy on my arm. I wasn't sure if he would stay quiet if I sat, and if he started squalling, I'd lose my chance to impress her further.

The woman folded the veil and set it on the seat beside her. "We haven't been properly introduced," she said. "I am Mrs. Nanette O'Halloran."

"I'm Bobby Lee Claremont. I'm going to Chicago to visit my aunt," I said. That lie was getting to be an easy habit. Then I remembered my manners, and how a person ought to talk to the bereaved. Lord knows, I'd heard it plenty lately, so I knew what to say.

"I'm sorry for your loss," I said. It sounded just as empty and useless as it had all the times folks had said it to me.

Her smile faded into sorrow. She nodded toward the baby on my arm. "It's him who's got it hard, having no daddy. He's the one I cry for."

Unexpectedly, I found my eyes stinging and my nose stuffing up. It surprised me—I hadn't cried when my mother got sick, or in the weeks I had nursed her and tried to help her get better. I hadn't even cried when the Sisters washed and dressed her or when they put her in the crypt. But somehow, holding this small, warm, vulnerable baby in my arms, and seeing the sadness in his mother's large black eyes, my own loss welled up until I was near to choking on it.

"I think he's asleep," I said, and thrust the baby back into his mother's arms, eager to be free of him. This wasn't what I had planned on at all. I couldn't convince anyone I was fit for a life of crime if I started blubbering over a baby.

She took the child, but she was looking me in the face. "You've lost someone too, haven't you."

I couldn't answer her; I couldn't trust my voice. I shrugged and looked out the window. I'd blown my chance. We sat in silence for a long moment while the train rocked us, along with the child.

"It helps to talk about it, you know," she said quietly. I didn't answer. She shifted the baby on her lap and gave a deep sigh.

"You never saw a fellow as full of life as my Jimmy," she said, her voice warm as she drew the words up out of memory.

"I'll never forget the first time I saw him, sitting at a table at the Crescent City Supper Club, close to the stage. I was performing that night with the Clovis Dupré Orchestra. I remember the very song I was singing."

She sang a few lines in a voice of velvet stitched with moonlight:

"Some of these days
You're gonna miss me, baby.
Some of these days
You're gonna find you're so lonely.

"And then our eyes met, and it was as if he'd caught me up in a spell. I couldn't look away. Oh, but he was handsome! And he had dreams! He was starting up a club of his own—the Cajun Queen Supper Club—right there in the heart of New Orleans. The world was our peach in those days, and nothing was going to stop us swinging from the moon if we wanted to!"

She was gazing out the window, a dreamy smile on her face. I felt a little dreamy too. I'd never been to those fancy clubs, knew nothing of the life she spoke of, but still she'd pulled me into that world.

She turned to me with a sigh, and her smile faded. We were back in the bleak present once again.

"I would trade all that now if it meant having my Jimmy back. If I had known that club would be the death of him and leave his own son a fatherless child . . . but there's no changing the past, is there. I suppose nothing that beautiful can last, except in memories."

"No, ma'am, I don't reckon it can," I replied. I had never

really known the kind of happiness she was talking about, but I knew that the happy moments were more fleeting than the troubles. Sister Mary Magdalene had told me troubles were sent by God to test our fortitude. I'd told her I didn't see why he had to give so darn many tests when he was supposed to know everything already.

"So now I'm leaving New Orleans, hoping to make a new life for my boy with his kinfolks in Chicago," Mrs. O'Halloran said. She looked down at the sleeping baby and stroked his cheek. "Is that why you're going to your aunt in Chicago too? Looking for a new family?"

I nodded. I had thought meeting her and quieting her baby was going to be the first step toward securing my future as a crook. But instead, she'd made me think of family and wholesome futures, with a hunger that pulled at my spine and ribs like a three-days-empty belly.

The train's whistle blew and the rhythm of the rails shifted as we began to slow. The woman smiled and placed a delicate, long-fingered hand on my knee.

"Whoever you've lost, hold on to your memories, Bobby Lee. Hold on to them real tight," she said. I looked at her hand on my knee, torn between throwing it off and holding it there forever.

The door at the end of the compartment opened and Sergeant Hayworth returned. Mrs. O'Halloran turned to look at him. He looked back at the two of us sitting together, his eyebrows raised. She removed her hand from my knee and straightened.

"Well," she said. "I suppose I should get back to my own

seat. Thank you kindly for your help. I hope you find what you're looking for in Chicago."

She gathered up her veil, situated the baby on her shoulder, and stood. She gave me one last wistful smile and returned up the aisle, leaving me alone, torn open by the raw ache of loss.

McCOMB, MISSISSIPPI 10:15 A.M.

It was midmorning when the train stopped in the small town of McComb for a few minutes. I stayed in my seat, but all three men traveling with Mrs. O'Halloran stepped off to stretch their legs and smoke on the platform. Mrs. O'Halloran tucked her still-sleeping baby into his basket on the floor beside her seat and went to the lavatory.

I was alone in the car, except for the baby and Sergeant Hayworth. I stole a glance his direction. He was leaning back in his seat, his hat over his face as if asleep. As quietly as I could, I slid across my seat until I was up against the dirty window. I wanted to see if the kid in the overalls was out there again, working the platform. I wanted to know what he was up to, and if there was a payoff in it.

I didn't see the boy, but I spotted the widow's companions right off. They stood in the dust outside the small, clapboard depot, looking a little uncomfortable. The small man in the pinstripes was lighting a cigar, cupping his hands around the flame as he did so, but his eyes were shifting back and forth between the others like he didn't trust them. Nobody was looking anybody in the eye. I took a page from the sergeant's book, closed my eyes, and leaned my head against the glass as if I were asleep. Unfortunately, with my eyes closed, I couldn't tell who was saying what, but I didn't want it to be obvious I was eavesdropping, so I resisted the urge to peek.

"I don't like it," said a husky voice.

"Keep your shirt on. There's nothing he can do now. He's Louisiana State Police, and we're in Mississippi," said a second voice, with a quick, pinched Yankee accent.

"He's out of his jurisdiction, but that don't mean there's nothing he can do," said the first voice, getting lower and huskier with disapproval. "I don't like it. I don't want to see Miss LeBlanc getting hurt."

"*Nom de Dieu!*" swore a third voice in Cajun French. "She ain't Miss LeBlanc anymore, Malcolm! How many times do I gotta tell you?"

"Sorry, boss. Mrs. O'Halloran. I just don't want to see Mrs. O'Halloran getting hurt."

I pressed a little harder against the glass. I didn't want her getting hurt either, even if I had only just met her.

"No one's getting hurt!" said the Yankee. "Just keep your mouths shut and your eyes open. She's got the insurance policy with her, she's got you as witnesses. Once she cashes out, we'll all be sitting pretty and there's nothing that cop can do. He's got nothing on any of us, and if nobody squeals, it'll stay that way."

"Don't worry, Mr. Kelly. We ain't gonna squeal, are we, Malcolm?" said the Cajun.

"Um. Sir?" said the husky voice that must have been Malcolm's. There was a silence then, broken by a shuffling, shifting sound on the dry earth, moving closer to the train. Then my nose prickled as a stream of cigar smoke came through the narrow opening in my window, right into my face. I sat up, coughing, and opened my eyes, only to see the three men gathered right below my window, glaring up at me. I gave them a quick smile, or the closest to it I could, what with my eyes and lungs burning. A smile that I hoped said "If you're a criminal, I surely would like a job!"

The small pin-striped fellow took a long drag on his cigar, his eyes regarding me with a steel-hearted chill. Off to their right a conductor called "All aboard!" and there was a scramble of passengers for the train, but the lean man didn't move. He just kept his blue eyes locked on mine and blew the smoke out of the corner of his mouth. My heart was racing, but I held his look with what I hoped was a steely gaze of my own. If I wanted to impress, I was going to have to start by showing a little grit.

Behind him, his two large companions were getting restless. "Come on, Kelly," said the Cajun, but Kelly just stood, his eyes still holding mine, his thin lips turning slowly up into a smile.

"Coming, Bujeau," he said, but he didn't move, or look away, or even blink. "Just remember what I said. Mouths shut and no one gets hurt." Then he leaned closer to the gap in the window and spoke right into it. "And if you're pretending to be asleep, don't squeeze your eyes shut quite so tight."

Then he crushed out his cigar with the heel of his shoe and strode to the door to board the car. All three men walked past my seat as they made their way up the aisle toward their own, but none of them even glanced my way. I watched their backs until they reached their seats. Then I turned my gaze away, not wanting them to see me staring as they sat down.

I glanced instead across the aisle to where Sergeant Hayworth still sat with his hat over his face. Somehow, though, I sensed he was smiling. It seemed everyone on this train car had seen right through me.

I turned my gaze back out the window as we rolled out of the station, past the squat houses and a sprawling sawmill. I watched it belch black smoke into the clear morning sky and tried to decide what to do. I'd gotten the criminals' attention, but not in the way I'd hoped. At least I was pretty sure they were criminals now, though I didn't exactly understand what they'd been talking about. Personally, I was all for the idea of nobody getting hurt, but the way that Yankee had said it, it sounded more like a threat than an assurance. And why had the big man called Mrs. O'Halloran Miss LeBlanc? Was she not really the widow of the dead man in the baggage car? An actress, perhaps, hired to scam the dead man's relatives? She had as much as told me she'd been on the stage, but her story had sounded—felt—true. And she had that baby.

No, I didn't think she was an actress. But something wasn't right, here. I thought back to the Yankee's words about insurance money. Suddenly, a new thought twisted hard in my belly: Mrs. O'Halloran's companions were somehow fixing to take advantage of her and her predicament! If that happened, her baby would surely grow up as I had, a burden to his mother as she went from job to job. My own mother had always hugged me and cried and told me I was her whole life whenever she lost another job. She'd quit because she missed me too much, she said. But I knew her dismissals were my fault. Folks wanted a cleaning lady who would put in long hours, not one who had to stop early to take care of a child, or worse yet, had the brat tagging along with her.

More than once Maman had found work as a domestic in one of the big houses on St. Charles Street, where they expected her there night and day. She'd leave me with the Sisters to take the job, but it would never last more than a month.

When I was little, I'd always been so happy when she came back. It wasn't until I was older that I understood she was giving up a warm, dry bed and three square meals a day so we could be a family—her, me, and a million cockroaches in a cheap room. If she hadn't come back to me, she wouldn't have gotten sick. And once she was sick, no one would hire her. No one wants a maid who's coughing up blood.

I wouldn't wish that on Mrs. O'Halloran. I had to protect her!

Then I remembered with a jolt why I was on this train to begin with. This was what criminals *did*. How was I going to get into a crime ring if I went all soppy at the sight of every widow I stumbled across? This was my big chance and I couldn't let it slip through my fingers.

I cleared my head and hardened my heart and thought again about what I had overheard. Something about an insurance policy that would cash out. I didn't rightly know what an insurance policy was, but I knew what cash was, and I knew that—whatever folks might say to the contrary—it could buy plenty of happiness. What I didn't understand was why it would have Mrs. O'Halloran's three companions sitting pretty, as that

Yankee, Mr. Kelly, had said. What right did they have to any insurance money?

Deep down, I knew the answer to my question: most likely they had no right. They were criminals, and they took what they wanted. And I admired that in them. But despite my efforts to harden my heart, it still didn't set right with me that their target was a widow and an orphan.

I tried to think of reasons I might be wrong about them until a wonderful possibility dawned on me. Maybe they were somehow stealing insurance money *for* Mrs. O'Halloran and her baby! In that case, they were *exactly* the sort of criminals I would want to fall in with. Being an orphan myself, it seemed to me that taking money from an insurance company to help a widow and her baby, and keeping a little on the side for yourself, was a nice way to profit all the way around.

Somehow or other, Mrs. O'Halloran and that baby were the key to all of this, and I reckoned that if I could speak to her privately, I could get her to tell me more. She'd sensed in me the kindred spirit of someone who'd lost a loved one. That connection had opened her heart and loosened her tongue. I was sure it would again. Then I'd know whether these were the criminals for me or not.

I glanced her way, wondering how I'd get her alone—only to discover that she was! Her companions had left the carriage while I had been lost in my thoughts. It was almost too easy.

I rose from my seat and strode with determination toward the widow, planning to plant myself in the seat opposite her, bold as anything. But just as I came up beside her seat, just as her eyes landed on mine and there was no going back, that pin-striped Yankee stepped through the door at the end of the carriage and stood not three paces away from us.

I must have blanched at the sight of him, because Mrs. O'Halloran's warm smile faltered and she turned, almost in alarm. When she saw who had surprised me, her smile became warm and comfortable once again.

"Oh, Bobby Lee, this is Mr. Brian Kelly. Mr. Kelly is an old friend of Jimmy's from Chicago. They grew up together. Mr. Kelly, this is Bobby Lee Claremont. He helped calm little Jimmy a while ago. He's got a fine touch with babies. Won't you sit down, Bobby Lee?"

I glanced again at Mr. Kelly. He looked back with hard eyes, his eyebrows lifting slightly in a question—*Well, kid, you've put your foot in it now. What are you going to do about it?* In answer, I gave Mrs. O'Halloran a smile, thanked her, and slid into the seat facing her. *Tell* that *to the crime bosses of Chicago, Brian Kelly. I've got nerves of steel!*

"What do you want, kid?" Kelly said, sliding into the seat next to the beautiful widow, whose big, dark eyes were asking the same question in a much kinder tone.

I swallowed and thought fast. I had been planning to just ask what had happened to her husband, but that was before Mr. Kelly had stepped into the plan.

"I—You—" My voice quavered, and I decided to use that to my advantage. I swallowed again, hard and obvious this time, like I was real choked up.

"It's just that you said it would help to talk," I said, turning my attention on the widow. "And you were right about me—I lost someone too. My mother. That's why I'm going to Chicago, to my aunt." Memories of Maman bobbed to the surface of my thoughts, and just like that, the lump in my throat was real, even though I'd meant to only be faking.

Mrs. O'Halloran's face was all compassion, her brow wrinkling and her eyes growing moist. "Oh, you poor boy!" she said, twisting her handkerchief between her hands. "You poor, poor boy. Here I've been so wrapped up in my own troubles, I never thought about what you were going through. How did she die?"

I closed my eyes for a moment and drew in an unsteady breath, seeing Maman again at the last, withered and coughing until she couldn't breathe—until she was choking on her own blood.

"Consumption," I said. "She'd been sick for nigh on a year."

"I'm so sorry," she said, and gave a deep, sad sigh. "At least I was spared the pain of seeing Jimmy weakened by illness. He was full of life to the last."

This was the opening I'd been looking for, and I jumped on it. "He was? What happened to him?"

"That's none of your business," Kelly said, but Mrs. O'Halloran put her hand on his arm in a gentle reprimand.

"No, it's okay," she said. "I don't mind saying. Jimmy fell, Bobby Lee. From a third-story window."

"How did he fall out a window?"

Her brow squeezed tighter, but she didn't draw back from the memory. "A rail on the balcony gave way. But never mind, you came to tell me about your mother. Was there nothing the doctors could do for her?"

I shook my head. "Couldn't afford a doctor," I said. "The Sisters of Charitable Mercy took care of her some, but there was not much they could do."

"What about your sister?" Mrs. O'Halloran asked.

"It was just me and Maman," I said. She gave me a curious look and I remembered the lie I'd told earlier. I felt my face redden. I was usually better at lying than this—lord knows I'd claimed to be everything from a choirboy to a soldier in the Salvation Army to separate sweet old ladies from their spare change—but talking of Maman's death had thrown me off.

"Truth is, I don't have a sister, ma'am. It was Sister Bernadette of the Charitable Mercies who taught me to take care of babies."

"I see," Mrs. O'Halloran said, smiling.

"What did I tell you," Brian Kelly burst in. "I don't believe a word of this tragic cock-and-bull story. His ma's probably a back-alley con, same as him. Unless he's a snitch for the cops."

"I am not!" I said, glaring at the sharp little Yankee. "I don't want anything to do with the cops. I just wanted to know how Mr. O'Halloran died, that's all. I felt bad, you know? Thinking you and the baby might end up like Maman and me, alone and poor. I thought maybe—maybe I could help!"

"How very kind of you, Bobby Lee," Mrs. O'Halloran said, putting a gentle hand on my knee. "Please don't mind Mr. Kelly. It's been so hard for all of us. It's very kind of you to be concerned, but you needn't be. We are taken care of."

I waited a moment for her to say more, but she didn't, so I put on a worried look. "Are you sure? It's just . . ." I hesitated, glancing at Mr. Kelly, who was still glaring at me. I hadn't convinced him I was a good kid, so I hoped I'd at least convinced him I was a decent con.

"Just what?" she asked gently.

"It's just that the policeman seems to think you might be in trouble. That's what he told me. I didn't ask, but that's what he said."

She smiled then, a wide, amused smile. "Oh, Bobby Lee. You are sweet. Here you've got so much trouble of your own, and you're worried about me."

"So you aren't in any trouble?" I ventured.

"Jimmy died in his club, so of course the police are investigating," Mrs. O'Halloran said.

"That's coppers for you, harassing honest citizens. Following us all the way to Chicago when he's got no right," Mr. Kelly growled.

"Now, Mr. Kelly—" Mrs. O'Halloran said mildly, but Kelly's face was turning crimson right to the roots of his hair.

"And now he's sent this kid over here, asking questions. They're trying to pin this on somebody, and they won't rest until they do. That's how coppers operate. They refuse to believe a railing broke by accident. 'He musta been pushed,' they say. 'Maybe there was a fight.' And then if they can't find the Charlie who actually pushed Jimmy, they have to think up something else. Maybe his widow had him bumped off to collect the life insurance. Maybe his childhood schoolmate has a secret grudge, and came all the way down from Chicago to shove him out a window. Is that what you're digging for, kid? Well, no dice. We're not telling you nothing. And you and your cop friend oughta keep away from Mrs. O'Halloran and me and our associates, understand?"

"Now, Mr. Kelly, Bobby Lee's got nothing to do with the police investigation, do you, Bobby Lee?" Mrs. O'Halloran said.

"I told you I didn't. I don't like the cops any more than you do," I said, trying to meet the challenge in Kelly's eyes.

"Well, since none of us have anything to hide, none of us have anything to fear." Mrs. O'Halloran said it bravely, but I could see the worry clumping up between her eyebrows.

Kelly glanced over at Hayworth, still situated a few rows away, and hatred flashed in his eyes. "That copper is doing more than his job, Nanette. He's following us clear out of his jurisdiction trying to trip us up. He ought to just get off this train and go back to where he belongs. It's not decent, hounding a grieving widow all the way to Chicago. It's hard enough taking Jimmy home without his interference. Or anyone else's," he added, cutting his sharp glance to me.

"I'm sorry to have intruded," I said, getting to my feet. Kelly's suspicion was too hot—I wouldn't learn anything more asking questions just now. Besides, I was pretty sure I had learned what I'd set out to learn. Mrs. O'Halloran was innocent, I felt positive of that. But as for Mr. Kelly—his ideas about the police were not the ideas of an innocent man. He had the heart of a criminal, I was more convinced of that then ever. But he was protective of Mrs. O'Halloran too. Maybe he *was* the kind of criminal I wanted to be. And if he was, I wanted to impress him. The only way I could think to do that now was with my discretion. I looked him square in the eye.

"I won't say a thing to that cop, Mr. Kelly. You can count on me. Now if you'll excuse me, I'm feeling thirsty," I said. "I think I'll go see what they're serving in the lounge car."

Mrs. O'Halloran nodded. "Thank you, Bobby Lee. You are a good boy."

A good boy. She wouldn't think so if she knew about my plans to become a first-rate crook in Chicago. Good folks didn't get ahead in this world. Being good to me was what killed Maman. I was done with good. So why did it warm my empty belly to hear her say it?

JACKSON, MISSISSIPPI
12:20 P.M.

I passed through the next car, and the next, making note as I went of the easy pickings along the way. The dozing lady with wax fruit on her hat and her pocketbook dangling open; the mother with too many children and no attention to spare for her luggage. Taking anything now with nearly twenty hours of travel still ahead of us wasn't a good idea, but it's always good to know the possibilities for later. Although, when I saw a silver cigarette case all but falling out of a napping man's pocket, I admit I helped liberate it. After all, someone so careless didn't deserve such a fine thing, and while I'd never tried smoking, I could see how it might be a good skill for a criminal to pick up.

I was picturing myself joining Kelly and his two cronies on the platform for a smoke when I stepped into the lounge car and came face to face with the cronies themselves. The sight of them jarred me out of my daydream and rooted me to the spot.

For a moment, we just stared at each other in silence. They were both big men—now that I was so close to them, I realized just how big—but they were big in different ways. The one who called Mrs. O'Halloran *Miss Le Blanc* was a massive wall of muscle and bone in a dull suit. The other was squarely built, but paunchy, as if the good life had been softening him up for a few years. His skin had a pasty, greasy look, as if he hadn't crawled out into the sunlight in a good long while. The muscular mountain of a man got to his feet, keeping his eyes on me.

"Boss?" he said, then waited for instructions.

The paunchy man smiled at me with a smile as oily as his skin. "Come on over, kid. We'd like a word with you."

The big man cracked his knuckles and I decided it wasn't a word I wanted to have just now. So I turned and hurried back the way I had come. I ducked into a lavatory in the next coach and waited, but after a few minutes peeking through the crack in the door, I decided they had not pursued. I wiped the sweat from my forehead and stepped back out.

I sat down in an empty seat in a different car, making myself invisible until we pulled into Jackson. Lots of folks were getting off to stretch their legs, so I did too. On the platform, the colored folks at the front of the train crowded a thin space near the engine, beyond the WHITES ONLY barrier, while the white folks spread out comfortably along the rest. Local vendors of both colors strolled among them, offering matches, newspapers, shoe shines, sandwiches, and candy. My stomach grumbled as I spied the food. It was lunchtime, and all I had eaten that day was the two corn pones that morning. I was feeling mighty empty.

I was eyeing the sandwiches and considering expanding my criminal qualifications, when Sergeant Hayworth stepped off the train. He glanced around in a way that said he didn't want to be seen, then strode across the platform and into the depot. There was no doubt from that look. He was up to something. I hadn't liked the slippery cop since the moment he'd first called me son, and seeing him trying to slither like a snake in the grass into the station didn't do much to raise my opinion of him. I forgot my empty stomach and followed to see where he was going.

Inside, the depot was crowded. All the doors and windows were open to let through a breeze, but the air was too damp and heavy to move. The ladies sitting on the benches looked flushed, even though they fanned themselves vigorously. The men had taken off jackets and loosened ties, but their faces still gleamed with sweat. The only folks with any spunk were a group of kids running in and out among the waiting travelers and generally kicking up a ruckus.

It took me a moment to locate the sergeant. He had barged in ahead of a whole line at the ticket counter to talk to the ticket agent. The folks in line were all glaring like he was a polecat in a henhouse, but I couldn't have been happier. I thought he was buying a ticket back to New Orleans. Soon, though, I saw I was mistaken. He wasn't buying anything. He spoke to the ticket agent for a moment, then the agent opened a door and the sergeant disappeared into the railroad office.

I didn't know what business he had in there, but I figured he'd be occupied for a spell, so I turned to the golden opportunity I'd seen in the crowded station. I looked around, locating my target. Then I strolled forward until I was in the path of the kids playing tag. When they came charging past, I let them sweep me up into the chase, shouting and laughing as I joined them. We went weaving through the crowd as if the devil himself was on our heels. Near the door to the platform, a lady was buying a paper from a boy, and her pocketbook was dangling open as she counted out pennies in her hand. As the crowd of kids flew past, I took a clumsy zag to the left and bumped her hard enough to jolt the coins out of her palm and a few more out of her open pocketbook.

I was a few steps past her before I could stop, which gave her time to get up a good head of steam.

"See here, you little hooligan!" she shouted.

"Sorry, ma'am," I said, turning back. I bent to help her gather up the coins and bobby pins that had spilled from her bag, while she continued to scold and complain. I kept muttering apologies, but I made no effort to quiet her. Upstanding ladies liked to indulge their indignation once in a while, and I was happy to oblige her. Once she was worked up, she wasn't so likely to notice that, while gathering up her spilled effects, I had placed my foot neatly atop a coin. I handed her back her things, apologizing yet again and promising to mend my ways. She chastised me one last time while I hung my head in remorse, then she marched away, her nose in the air.

When she was gone, I squatted down to tie my shoelace—and to scoop up the coin beneath my foot. I slid my foot sideways to reveal a whole quarter. It was my lucky day! I picked it up and took a moment to enjoy the weight of it on my palm before I slipped it into my pocket. Then I straightened. A glance back over my shoulder showed me Sergeant Hayworth emerging from the railroad office. I figured that was my signal to head for the train. No point being in the station should the lady realize she had lost some money.

"You're one smooth operator," a voice said as I stepped out onto the platform. I turned toward the compliment, hoping it had come from one of the crooks in my car. Maybe he'd seen my con and wanted to take me under his wing! But instead, it was only the two colored boys who'd helped me up, back in New Orleans. They were taking one heck of a risk. They were on the narrow section of the platform where whites and blacks mingled between their separate cars and separate waiting rooms, but the boys were dangerously close to the entrance to the whites-only area. Not that it bothered me none, but there were plenty of white folks who could take offense. And things never came out so good for black folks once white folks took offense, far as I could tell.

The older boy was leaning against the depot wall beside the door, his hands tucked into his overall bib. The younger one, Terrance, was grinning ear to ear.

"Beg pardon?" I said. Innocence was my best defense if they were thinking of turning me in.

"Does your Yankee aunt know you're a thief?" the older kid said.

"I don't know what you're talking about," I said, and I began walking toward the train, stiff-backed and indignant. I was plenty annoyed. I had planned to use my money to buy sandwiches from the carts on the platform, but I didn't dare show the money now, not in front of two boys ready to make a scene. Not when Sergeant Hayworth himself had just come out onto the platform. If it came to my word against theirs, white against black, I had the advantage, unfair as that was. But there was no point in pushing my luck.

Terrance began trotting along after me.

"Don't be sore!" he said. "I think if you're gonna be an operator, you ought to be a smooth one. Least that's what our pop says. Can you teach me how to do that?"

I shrugged and kept walking. "Ain't nothing to teach you, 'cause I ain't done nothing," I said, falling into the comfortable street talk Sister Mary Magdalene so strongly objected to, but was more fitting for a shady character such as myself.

Out of the corner of my eye, I could see Sergeant Hayworth angling across the platform toward the same door as me. I certainly didn't want to arrive at that door at the same time as a copper, while trailing a little kid who was jabbering on about smooth operators. So, I stopped walking and turned to the boy. To my surprise, his older brother had trailed along too, a few steps behind us. I glared at them both.

"What do you want from me?" I said quietly, making sure my back was toward Hayworth so he wouldn't see or hear what I was saying. I was hoping he just wouldn't notice me, but if he did, I wanted him to think we were just a bunch of kids, playing together. Of course, I had outgrown child's play, but it was a safe thing for Hayworth to assume.

The older boy grinned, a little wickedly. "Well, now, that's a mighty good question," he said. "For starters, me and Terrance here are getting a little hungry. It's lunchtime."

"So buy yourself a sandwich," I said, waving toward one of the sandwich carts on the platform.

"Can't," the younger boy said. "That's for white folks only."

"Which is where you come in," the older boy said.

I eyed him coolly. "Seems to me *you're* the smooth operator here. I saw you go into the baggage car and not come back out in Hammond. I suppose you were stealing back there too."

He stiffened and his grin wilted away. "I was working," he said.

"Yeah? I don't see anyone else your age working for the Illinois Central."

"You won't tell, will you?" little Terrance said.

"Hush up, Terrance," his brother said. "Ain't nothing to tell. I was working."

"And I am just taking the air," I said, challenging him with my look. I glanced over my shoulder. Hayworth had stopped and was talking to someone near the door to our train carriage. I still couldn't get by him without being seen. I had to lose these boys, and quick.

The older boy followed my glance, and, seeing my expression, jumped once again to the offensive.

"You nervous?" he asked.

"Why should I be nervous?" I tried to sound casual, but he wasn't buying it.

"That there is the long arm of the law. And you're keeping a mighty close eye on him for someone who ain't done nothing. Maybe me and Terrance should go have a word with him."

The threat had been meant for me, but the younger boy crowded against his brother, gripping his hand.

"I don't want to talk to no policeman, Leon. Don't make me."

"And maybe I should tell him about you being in the baggage car," I said.

Leon shrugged, but I could see I had him. I didn't know what his story was, but I was sure now it wasn't on the up-and-up. He wouldn't talk to the cop. I'd called his bluff.

"We won't tell the copper nothing, will we, Leon?" Terrance said. "We want to be friends is all."

"Then why are you trying to shake me down?" I said, still glaring at Leon.

He glared back. We stood like that for several seconds before the train whistle blew, warning everyone it was time to get on board. All around us, passengers began to surge toward the train.

Leon broke eye contact first, turning to Terrance and taking his hand. "See, I told you it was a bad idea. We're better off on our own. We don't need some guttersnipe from the Quarter to have fun. Come on." Together they started forward, toward the colored cars at the front of the train, but Terrance pulled his hand free and turned to me.

"We're sorry. We didn't mean nothing by it," he said in a plaintive voice, his eyes going big and irresistibly sweet as he looked up at me through his long, curving lashes. He was a smooth operator too, by the looks of things. And from their accent, I could tell that they weren't exactly from the best ward in New Orleans, either. "You should come eat lunch with us. We've got a prospersition for you, right, Leon?

"Proposition," Leon corrected him.

"Come join us in the lounge car," Terrance persisted. "It's that one there." He pointed to the last car in the Negro section of the train.

"I can't eat in the colored car," I said.

"Sure you can," Terrance said. "The food's just fine, and it's cheaper than what they serve in the white folks' dining car. Granddaddy says that's the best-kept secret on the Illinois Central."

"I ain't colored," I pointed out, though it was as plain as the freckled nose on my face. Leon had guessed right; my mother was from the French Quarter, and though I knew nothing about my daddy, my skin was too fair and my hair too sandy for him to have been a Creole or a Negro.

"Just tell 'em Leon and Terrance sent you," Leon said. "If you want to hear our proposition, that is. I don't care one way or the other. Come on, Terrance."

With that, he took the little boy's hand more firmly and led him off toward the colored cars.

Relieved to be free of them, I turned back toward my own car, hurrying as I did. I nearly collided with Sergeant Hayworth at the train steps.

"Well, hello, son. Taking the air, were you?" the sergeant said.

"Yes, sir. And you?"

He nodded and patted his pink, sweaty forehead with his handkerchief. "I think it's going to be a hot one. You're wise to enjoy it while you can, before the heat gets to be too much, if you know what I mean," he said.

I didn't know exactly. But from the cold smirk he gave me as he mounted the steps to our car, I wasn't sure I wanted to find out.

CANTON, MISSISSIPPI
12:56 P.M.

I couldn't deny that I was hungry—not with the way my stomach was grumbling—and as much as they annoyed me by calling me out, I was curious about Terrance and Leon's so-called proposition. But I wasn't about to go eat in the colored people's car.

I had nothing against colored people; in fact, I liked what I'd seen of them on this train a far cry better than some of the white folks I'd become acquainted with. I figured colored folks were just folks, same as anyone else. Sister Mary Magdalene had often reminded me we were all equal in the eyes of God. Which didn't quite explain the lot God had given colored folks. Maybe their fortitude needed extra testing, or maybe the good Sister had been wrong, because it didn't seem to me their separate was all that equal, or one bit fair. But fair or not, I was old enough to know who to associate with if I wanted to get on in the world. To a lot of upstanding white folks, associating with Negroes could taint a fellow quicker than almost anything. And if I was in a train car with members of Chicago's underworld, I didn't want to do anything that would give them a bad impression of me. I wanted them to see that I could be bad in the best possible way. Hobnobbing with a couple of Negro kids might give them the impression that I wasn't of the right caliber.

So, as the train pulled out from Jackson, I stayed put—in my own seat, in my own car, with my stomach rumbling. After a while, Mrs. O'Halloran and her acquaintances rose from their seats and disappeared toward the back of the train, where the whites-only dining car was located. The cop waited about thirty seconds before he followed, leaving me alone.

I sighed and flopped down across my seat, letting my feet hang out into the aisle. If I was going to have to stay hungry until the next stop with sandwich carts, I might as well get comfortable, I thought, closing my eyes.

I must have drifted off because the next thing I knew, a big hand was on my ankle and giving it a shake. I jerked upright so quick, I banged my head on the window frame. One of Nanette O'Halloran's companions, the big soft one, had hold of me, and I was suddenly regretting having run from him earlier. He stepped closer, blocking my path to the aisle, and all but pressed his expansive gut into my face so that I was eye to eye with a gaudy, ruby-studded watch chain that stretched across his vest. I forced my eyes up, to his greased-back hair and his small, dark eyes, which were glaring down at me.

"What do you want?" I said. It came out in a squeal, sounding like a stuck pig, but I couldn't help it. He'd caught me by surprise.

He gave a little snort of a laugh, sounding piglike himself. "Well now, *mon ami*, it's not what I want, it's what you want. That's what I've come to discuss," he said, his quick, rhythmic Cajun accent sounding straight off the bayou.

"What I want?" I repeated in surprise. I wanted an in with the gangsters. I wanted to walk into the headquarters of the Chicago mob, offer my services, and start raking in the dough. But I didn't see how this Cajun dandy was going to get that for me. So I decided to let him talk and see if he gave me any ideas. I shrugged and tried to look innocent.

"Everyone wants something. In my line of work, I see it every day," he said.

"Your line of work?" I repeated.

He straightened, which made the buttons strain on his expensive vest. "You're looking at the proprietor of the Cajun Queen Supper Club," he said, meaning to impress.

"Yeah? I thought Jimmy O'Halloran owned the Cajun Queen."

He deflated a little, eyeing me with annoyance. "We were partners, but never mind that. What is it you want, kid? What are you after?"

I smiled, trying to project more bravado than I felt. "I want it all."

He gave a bark of laughter, followed by a few choice French curse words.

"So now that I've told you what I want," I said, trying to be cool and slick, "what is it that *you* want?"

"You haven't told me anything," he said, his face getting serious and threatening again. "Come on, kid, out with it. First you eavesdrop, then you follow us and run away when we spot you. What's your scheme?"

I shrugged again. I didn't want to admit that the sight of him and his enormous, knuckle-cracking associate earlier in the day had scared me. So I used the first excuse that came to mind. "Mr. Kelly told me to keep my distance, that's all," I said.

At once, his eyes narrowed down into slits. "Oh he did, did he? To keep away from *me*, did he? And why did he tell you to do that?"

I hesitated, unsure what to say. I'd hit a deeper nerve than I'd been angling for when I'd mentioned Kelly.

"Don't play dumb with me, kid. What did that little Irish weasel tell you while I had my back turned?" His heavy jowls were turning red and a cowlick over his forehead had broken free from its heavy grease job and was bobbing over his forehead like a rooster's comb.

I glanced sideways. I could probably escape over the seats if he got violent. He didn't seem all that agile. So I decided to see what I could get from him, keeping my escape route in mind should I push too far.

"Kelly didn't tell me anything, Mister . . . Mister . . . what's your name, anyway?"

"Bujeau," he said, a little grudgingly. "Alphonse Bujeau."

I raised my eyebrows as if I knew something. "Oh, so *you're* Alphonse Bujeau!"

"I didn't kill him!" Bujeau blurted, little beads of spittle accompanying his words into my face.

"No?" I said, mildly, as if I might or might not believe him. If there was one thing I'd learned around the Sisters, it was how to be noncommittal.

"I'm not the only one who had something to gain by Jimmy's death, you know!" he growled. "But I didn't *want* the Cajun Queen to myself. Jimmy was the life of that place, and I respected that, even if I didn't always agree with him. And Nettie's all set to profit too, if that life insurance pays out, did they tell you that? No, they wouldn't, would they."

"And Mr. Kelly? How would he profit?" I asked.

His eyes narrowed again and he drew in a deep breath as he suddenly seemed to realize how loose his tongue had gotten. "Brian Kelly's a Yankee. Remember that before you go puttin' stock in him. He shouldn't even be here, far as I can see."

"Why is he, then?" I asked.

"You know what they say. *Où il y a des os, il y a des chiens.*"

It was a common expression in the Quarter: where there are bones, there are dogs. Maman had often said it to remind me not to trust the folks who were suddenly friendly when I had something to offer. Was that what Mr. Kelly was doing with Mrs. O'Halloran? Was her insurance policy the bone he was after, or was *she*? Mrs. O'Halloran hadn't seemed ready to be thinking of another man. If there was one thing I felt sure of, it was that she loved her Jimmy and was in no state to be wooed. But Mr. Kelly might be hoping to make himself the first man she'd think of when she was ready.

"If I were you . . ." Bujeau's eyes strayed toward the door at the far end of the train and his expression stiffened. Without another word, he turned and headed down the aisle. I watched him go. When he opened the door and passed through to the platform between the cars, I saw a flash of brown. I leaned out into the aisle to see better. Sergeant Hayworth was standing there, smoking a cigarette. His eye caught mine briefly as Bujeau stormed past him, and he smiled at me. Not a friendly smile. More an *I caught you in the act* kind of smile, which made my insides squirm. He kept smiling until he'd finished his cigarette. Then he flicked the butt off the train and followed Bujeau into the next car.

I wished Bujeau had been able to finish his sentence. Still, it had been a useful conversation, I decided, once I got over my initial fright. I knew a few things now. First, Bujeau had no love for Kelly, not that there was any great surprise there. Kelly was about as likable as a cockroach in your jambalaya. But judging by Bujeau's sweat and the way his little piggy eyes had dilated, he feared Kelly too.

Second, Bujeau wasn't much good at holding his tongue.

Third, as much as I wished it weren't true, Kelly was out to get something from Mrs. O'Halloran, as I had originally suspected.

And finally, Bujeau was afraid of having Jimmy O'Halloran's death pinned on him. Did that confirm that Jimmy's death was murder? Not necessarily. But it did confirm that Bujeau seemed as skittish as a hare, and not much smarter than one.

Kelly, on the other hand, seemed awfully smart when compared to Bujeau. And unlikable as he was, he was more interesting than ever. Maybe getting in with him wasn't the worst idea. If I did, maybe then I wouldn't have to work my way to the head office of the mob in Chicago after all. Maybe Kelly was the man who could take me straight there. And maybe, by getting in with Mr. Kelly, maybe that was the best way for me to look out for Mrs. O'Halloran too.

Applying for a job with a gangster wasn't something to attempt on an empty stomach. I thought again of Terrance and Leon's offer. I could sneak up to the colored car now and no one would be the wiser. So I stood, straightened my shabby coat, and strode forward in search of lunch.

The colored folks' lounge car was noisy and packed with people. In the back corner, a group of old men were gathered around a table playing penny-ante poker. Families were gathered here and there along the length of the narrow car, talking, laughing, teasing. Little girls sat on the floor together, playing with rag dolls. A counter in the corner opposite the card players offered food and drink. Several porters, looking much more relaxed than those I'd seen in other parts of the train, were serving up plates of food from pots and kettles behind the counter. I could smell the aromas from where I stood in the doorway. The warmth of family tugged at my heart and the food at my taste buds, and before I knew it, I was pulled into the car and making for the line at the food counter.

I was aware of people glancing my way and whispering as I walked the length of the car. I didn't belong there, white as I was and standing out like a sore thumb, but with no sign of Leon and Terrance, all I could think to do was try to put on an innocent face, like a little kid who could still mix without reproach.

There was a short line at the counter. I took my place politely at the back, but everyone shifted aside and let me through to the counter first. They gave me grudging looks as I stepped up, which seemed a little unfair. I hadn't asked for any favors. But I reckoned it also wasn't fair that my skin color gave me privileges, even here in the car reserved for them.

The porter behind the counter, who had seemed so relaxed

when I spotted him from the doorway, stiffened at the sight of me and checked to make sure his jacket was buttoned.

"Can I help you, sir?" he said.

"I think they were first," I said, pointing to the folks who had let me by.

He shook his head. "What can I do for you, sir? Is there somethin' needs cleanin' up in your car? I'll get right on it."

"No, sir. I would like to order lunch."

The porter looked amused and a little embarrassed at that. "You've come to the wrong place, sir. Your dining car's toward the back of the train. That's where you'll be wanting lunch."

I glanced at the pot behind the counter and the greasy green mass floating in it. I'd seen plenty of pots like that when I was doing odd jobs in the poor parts of town.

"It's just that I got a hankering for fatback and collard greens, and Terrance and Leon invited me to come up here for some," I said.

Behind me I heard a woman say, "Well, I'll be," and another replied, "If that don't beat all."

"Does your momma know you're here?" the porter asked.

"My momma's not on the train—nor my daddy. I'm on my own. Are Terrance and Leon here?"

The porter grumbled, but he heaped a pile of greens onto a plate, making sure I got a big hunk of the fatback in it. Then he added corn bread, fried hominy, and some cracklins. It was the biggest plate of food I'd seen in days, and the whole thing only cost me a nickel.

I paid and looked around the car for a place to sit and eat. My eyes went to an empty bench at a table in the corner. I liked corners, where I could be out of sight and out of mind, but there was no chance of my being invisible here. As I made my way to the empty seat, the ladies seated on the opposite bench picked up their plates and moved, though there were no other open seats in the car. With a twinge of guilt, I tried to tell them that it wasn't necessary, but they pretended not to hear, so I took my seat and dug into my food. I suppose most kids my age would have objected to eating all those greens, but I had long since learned not to object to anything that would fill my innards. I would have enjoyed my lunch more, though, if everybody hadn't kept staring at me. When I looked up from my plate, their eyes slid off me like butter off hot corn, but I could feel their minds still turned my way. The room had taken on a restrained feeling, as if all the love and laughter they'd been sharing had to be hidden away from me. Terrance and Leon still didn't seem to be anywhere in the crowd. I guessed they had given up on me, or hadn't been serious to start with. I began shoveling the food into my mouth as fast as I could, eager to get out of the car and back to my own.

"You eat like you ain't seen food in a week."

I looked up to see both boys standing by the table, watching me. I had no idea where they'd come from.

"I bet he ain't," said Leon. "Told you he was a guttersnipe. I bet you don't even have an aunt in Chicago. I bet you got nobody."

"Do so," I said, still shoveling greens into my mouth. "She's got a fine, big place up there. Servants, and feather beds, and everything."

Leon grinned and nodded, in a way that said he didn't

believe a word of it. "Does this Yankee aunt of yours like collard greens as much as you do?"

"Don't know. I ain't never stayed with her before. That's why I figure I got to get my fill of them now," I said, challenging his smile with an even bigger one of my own.

Terrance giggled. "You've got greens stuck atween your teeth," he said. "Can I have some of your cracklins?" With that, he sat down in one of the seats the women had vacated, and Leon followed. I turned my plate and let Terrance help himself.

"So I bet you wanna hear our prospersition now, don't you?" Terrance said, grinning so big his round cheeks bunched up into dimples.

"Proposition," Leon corrected. His look was still a little hostile, but I was beginning to suspect he was more bark than bite.

"Not really," I said.

"Yes you do," Terrance said, still grinning. "'Member the coffin you saw when you got on the train? Well, we're gonna find out who's in that coffin and we're gonna let you help us, right, Leon?"

I looked at Leon. "Is that why you were in the baggage car before? Trying to figure out who's dead in that box?" I asked.

"I told you, I was in the baggage car because I was working. Loading the mail."

"Mm. I see. Well, I already know who's in the coffin," I said.

"You do?" Terrance's face lit up like Bourbon Street on Mardi Gras.

I gave them a sly smile and took a big bite of corn bread, chewing slow and deliberate.

"And?" said Leon when it was obvious I wasn't going to say anything else.

"You've got access to the baggage car, why don't you see for yourself?" I said.

"We already tried that," Terrance said.

"You tried opening the *coffin*?"

"No! We figured the coffin's traveling with that widow. So we went into the baggage car and looked for a name on her trunk. It's new, and mighty fancy, with the initials N. O. on the lock. That's all we found out," said Leon.

"So who is it?" Terrance asked. "We know you're in the same car with the widow. What's N. O. stand for?" He was bouncing up and down in his seat with anticipation, and his excitement got the better of me.

"The dead man's a fellow named Jimmy O'Halloran," I said.

At once, both Terrance's and Leon's eyes grew wide.

"*The* Jimmy O'Halloran?" Leon asked.

"You know him?"

"Well sure!" Terrance said. "But that can't be his widow in your car."

"It is. Nanette O'Halloran," I said.

"But—"

"Hush up, Terrance," Leon said sharply. I started to ask Terrance what he was going to say, but then the whole lounge car went silent. I looked up. There stood three white men—Alphonse Bujeau, Mr. Kelly, and their knuckle-cracking companion, all glaring around at the crowd. Then they spotted me and headed my way.

Leon practically jumped out of his seat, grabbing a handful

of Terrance's shirt on the way. Slick as gators on a riverbank, they slipped into the crowd and disappeared. I looked up at the three men and tried to smile. They didn't smile back. Had Bujeau talked to Kelly and discovered I'd tricked him into telling me more than he ought? I had a feeling it was all about to come out, but what exactly *it* was, I couldn't say. I was just glad Nanette O'Halloran wasn't there. I figured I was about to either declare my intention to be a crook or get pounded before I could do so, and I was glad that whichever it was going to be—and I'd know in a matter of seconds—she wouldn't be there to see it.

DURANT, MISSISSIPPI
1:40 P.M.

The train slowed as it rolled through the small town of Durant, Mississippi, but my heart sped up as Alphonse Bujeau and Brian Kelly sat down at my table. The third man, the walking mountain, stood behind them and folded his arms. His biceps bulged and strained the stitches in his jacket till they were fit to burst. I admit, they strained my nerves a bit too. And I wasn't the only one. The colored folks around us had all eased away as far as they could. If these men were here because I had offended, no one was going to come to my aid. I swallowed and tried to smile.

Bujeau and Kelly gave me the once-over. I waited. After all, they'd come to me, so I figured it was their place to start the talking.

Kelly spoke first. He had been glaring at me with those narrow Yankee eyes, but soon they cut sideways to Bujeau and he grumbled, "Get on with it."

Bujeau shot Kelly a venomous look. *"Bec mon l'chu!"* he muttered. Kelly didn't react. I guess he didn't speak enough French to know what Bujeau had just told him to kiss. That did make me smile, but not for long, because Bujeau glared at me. "I just had a little conversation with my associate here, who tells me he found you sweet-talking Nanette earlier. Trying to get information from her. It's time to spill it, kid. We know you talked to that copper as soon as you boarded the train, and again just now, before we left Jackson. For the last time, who are you working for?"

I guessed Bujeau thought he could get more out of me if he presented a united front with Kelly. I shrugged, hoping I could impress Kelly with my coolness and trick Bujeau into telling me more. "What's it to you?" I said. The big man standing behind the others shifted his feet a little wider apart, which somehow made him even bigger. A trickle of sweat escaped my hairline and slid down into my collar.

"That's it. The kid's working for the cop," said Kelly.

"I told you before. I don't work for cops," I said, letting him see how the very idea offended. "In fact, I would like to work—"

"If you ain't working for the cop, why'd you get so chummy with him right off the bat?" Bujeau asked, his paunchy face red and sweaty like a gumbo pot fixing to boil over.

I glared at his interruption. "I was hungry. He offered me food. I let him think I was innocent while I ate his corn pones."

"And what favor did you promise him in return for your breakfast?" Kelly asked.

"He didn't ask for any favors, and even if he had, I wouldn't have done it. I'm no snitch."

"In my experience, nothing in life is free," Kelly said, his words cool and professional. If Bujeau was like a pot boiling over, Kelly was like an iceberg. The one that sank the *Titanic*. "If that fine officer of the law gave you breakfast, there were strings attached. We just want to know what they were."

"Admit it, kid," Bujeau growled. "You're in that copper's hip pocket for sure."

"I am not!" I wanted to be cool like Kelly, but I could feel the blood rising to my cheeks. On the streets of New Orleans, there was no lower creature than a snitch, working for the cops. "I told you already, the cops are no friends of mine!" I said.

Kelly looked me up and down again, finishing with a long, hard look into my eyes, his icy gaze worming into my soul for the truth. He meant to make me squirm, but he didn't stand a chance. Not after all the practice Sister Mary Magdalene had given me.

"He doesn't have anything going with the police, Alphonse," Kelly said at last. My heart soared—at least until he added, "The kid's nothing to us."

"But we've got to make sure!" Bujeau burst in. I noticed he was sweating. "Look, kid. There's two hundred dollars in it for you if you keep your mouth shut. What do you say to that?" He pulled a thick roll of bills from his pocket and flashed it in front of me.

My mouth fell open. I hurried to snap it shut. I had never dreamed of so much money. I swallowed to prime my voice, which had dried up like a quince in the sun.

"Two hundred? Just to keep my mouth shut?" This was going to be the easiest money I'd ever made. Since all I really knew about these men was what I'd overheard them saying on the platform back in McComb, and I didn't even rightly understand *that*, there really *was* nothing I could spill to Sergeant Hayworth. But Bujeau didn't need to know that.

Kelly, on the other hand, seemed to guess as much. "Bujeau,

you fool!" Kelly said. "I told you, he's got nothing. You're wasting your money."

"It's a deal!" I said quickly, before Kelly could convince Bujeau otherwise. Parting a fool from his money was the first trick any criminal worth his salt learned, and I was happy to show Kelly I knew how. "My lips are sealed, you can count on me. And if you need—"

"You better believe your lips are sealed, *maudit enfant*!" Bujeau said. "Because if I see one sign of you betraying Nan to those coppers, I'll be very unhappy. And when I get unhappy, Malcolm here gets unhappy." He jabbed a thumb back over his shoulder at the wall of man behind him. Malcolm cracked his knuckles. A vein jumped and throbbed in his thick neck.

I swallowed hard. I didn't know what he thought I might betray about Nanette, but I wasn't going to let him see my ignorance. So I smiled, turning my gaze to Bujeau, then Kelly, then Bujeau again. "Well, if there's anything else I can do for y'all, anything at all—"

Bujeau made a deep noise of disapproval in his throat and grabbed me by the collar. He pulled my face right up to his. His breath was warm and heavy with garlic and onions as he hissed, "*Mets pas ton doigt entre l'arbre et l'écorce, n'est-ce pas?*" It was an old Cajun expression, and sage advice: don't put your finger between the tree and the bark.

"Beg pardon, Mr. Bujeau, but does there seem to be some kind of trouble here?" said a deep, rich voice, new to the conversation.

Bujeau released my collar and I fell back into my seat, breathing hard. Everyone turned to see four Negro men standing by the table. Three of them stood a bit farther back, looking nervous. The fourth stood closer, his stance loose and easy. He was a large man with broad shoulders and big hands, though he still looked small next to Bujeau's thug. The relief I had felt when Bujeau let go of my collar faltered. This man couldn't do anything for me with three white men opposing him. He had to be crazy to even try. He smiled a broad, friendly smile at Bujeau. A gold-capped eyetooth caught the light, and everyone's attention.

Terrance was hovering just to the side of the new arrivals, also grinning like a lunatic. Apparently, he had something to do with getting this man involved. I didn't know whether to thank him or kick him. I had been on the verge of getting on the payroll of a real, live criminal. Sure, Bujeau and not Kelly, the man I really needed to impress. And true, I might have been about to be roughed up. But it was a first step, and one that could earn me two hundred dollars!

Bujeau smiled up at the new arrival. "Well, hello, Clovis. Boys," he said, nodding first to the speaker and then his companions. "We were just having a bit of a chat with young Bobby Lee here, about his intentions regarding Mrs. O'Halloran."

The man called Clovis started a little and looked at me with surprised amusement. "This boy has intentions regarding Mrs. O'Halloran? Seems to me as he's a little young for that."

"I ain't got intentions about nobody!" I said, feeling sore at Bujeau for threatening me and at this Clovis fellow for interrupting.

"You can leave him here with me and I'll keep an eye on him for you, Mr. Bujeau. Y'all go on back to your own car with no worries. That way no one has to feel too uncomfortable 'bout mixing where they oughtn't to, if you catch my meaning."

Bujeau glanced around uncomfortably and stood, understanding that Clovis was coming as near as a colored man dared to throwing them out.

Kelly didn't seem to understand that. Or to care. "Say, that's a swell idea," he said, eyeing me sharply. "If you keep the kid back here, he can't say nothing to the cops. That'll sure save you a few dollars, Bujeau."

"But we had a deal!" I protested.

Bujeau grinned and tucked the roll of money back into his pocket.

Kelly dipped a hand into his trouser pocket, turning toward Clovis as he did. "You keep a good eye on him, boy. You understand me?" He pulled a quarter from his pocket and flipped it at Clovis. Clovis shifted to let the coin sail past him and clatter on the floor. The crowded car rustled with disapproval.

"Let's go," Kelly said to Bujeau, and they walked toward the door, trailing the hulking Malcolm—and my best chance to become part of the criminal element—behind them.

WINONA, MISSISSIPPI
2:24 P.M.

"Why'd you have to go and do that?" I demanded, as I watched Bujeau and his big roll of money disappear through the door. Terrance was still smiling a proud, crooked smile.

"If that widow is Nanette O'Halloran, I thought you'd want to meet Clovis Dupré. He knows Nanette from way back, don't you, Clovis."

"Sure do," Clovis Dupré said, flashing that gold tooth again.

"Well you didn't have to run them off!"

Mr. Dupré—or Clovis, as everyone seemed to call him—chuckled as he and the other men sat down uninvited at my table.

"Looked to me like you needed a bit of help."

"I had them right where I wanted them," I grumbled.

"In my experience, everyone needs a bit of help now and then," Clovis said mildly, as if he hadn't heard me. "It takes a big man to admit it and accept it with grace."

"You sound like a nun," I said.

He only chuckled again.

I turned to Terrance. "Before those men came in here, we were talking about Jimmy O'Halloran and Nanette. How do you know about them?" I asked.

"Everybody who knows jazz knows them," Terrance said, looking at me like he couldn't believe I was so ignorant. "Don't you know nothing about jazz?"

I shrugged. Truth was, I didn't, but I sure wasn't going to let a little kid like Terrance think he knew more than me. One time, one of the boys at the orphanage had come up with a jazz record and we'd snuck into Sister Evangeline's room to listen to it on her gramophone. But I hadn't heard more than a few bars before she'd caught us and dragged us by our ears to Sister Mary Magdalene, who gave us each a dozen Hail Marys and a week scrubbing floors for our trouble. Jazz, according to the good Sisters, was the devil's music. Meaning I was plenty sure I'd like it, if I ever got a chance to actually hear it.

I turned back to the small circle of men at the table. I could see now that their hands were soft—not the hands of manual laborers—and suddenly Clovis's name and Mrs. O'Halloran's wistful words about performing in front of Jimmy came back to me. "So y'all must be the Clovis Dupré Orchestra?"

Clovis's grin widened and his gold tooth flashed as he glanced at his companions. "You hear that, boys? We're famous."

The other men at the table laughed, but I ignored them. I wanted answers.

"Then you've known Mrs. O'Halloran since before she met her husband—when she was singing with you," I said.

He nodded. "That's right. And I'm wondering what sorts of intentions a young fellow such as yourself might have toward the widow O'Halloran."

"None at all," I said.

"None at all. Well now." Clovis grinned. "I expect that makes you about the only fella in that car back yonder who can make that claim."

"Do you mean because of the insurance?" I asked.

"You sure know a lot for someone with no intentions," Clovis observed.

"What's insurance?" Terrance asked.

Clovis smiled at Terrance and ruffled his hair—or more accurately, his head, since Terrance's hair was cropped so short he was nearly bald. "How about you take that quarter off the floor and get us some coffee and corn bread?" he said.

"But what's insurance?" Terrance asked again, to my relief. I wanted Dupré to answer him so I wouldn't have to ask.

"Money the widow gets to help take care of her if her husband dies," Clovis said. "It's something for wealthy folks."

Terrance's brow wrinkled up in confusion.

"But—"

"You can get yourself some cracklins too," Clovis said.

Terrance's face lit up. "Thank you, Mr. Dupré," he said, and skipped off to the food counter, lickety-split.

Clovis turned back to me, his face serious. "She told you she was getting the money?"

I gave a half shrug, not wanting to admit my source. "Not exactly."

"Did she tell you about the future she would have had with us?" said one of the band members, who had been quiet until then.

"Now, Lou," Clovis said. "Ain't no point in digging up old ghosts."

"'Course not," said the man called Lou, who got to his feet. "Come on, fellas."

The other men followed his lead, and soon I was alone with Clovis.

He turned back to me. "What do you know about the insurance money?" he asked again.

"Only that there is some. I figure Mrs. O'Halloran is counting on it now that she ain't got a husband to take care of her and the baby."

He raised his eyebrows. "Has it occurred to you that Jimmy and Alphonse were partners?"

"Mr. Bujeau may have said something about that," I hedged.

"Then has it occurred to you that by rights, Nettie should own half of the Cajun Queen, as Jimmy's widow?"

It most certainly hadn't occurred to me. Now I felt a wave of relief, thinking of the income the club would give her. She could raise her baby right, send him to proper schools, feed him proper meals, keep her own health. But a question nagged at me.

"If she owns the Cajun Queen, why is she leaving New Orleans? She doesn't need Jimmy's kinfolks in Chicago. She'll be set up finer than frog's hair in New Orleans."

"It's a bit more complicated than that, I'm afraid," Clovis said. "I've heard there's some difficulty about the matter of a marriage license. The great state o' Louisiana seems to have . . . misplaced it."

"You mean she and Jimmy weren't really married?" I was shocked. "But they were in love! And she has his son! They *must* have been married."

Terrance arrived back at the table with the corn bread, coffee, cracklins, and Leon.

Clovis leaned back in his chair and picked up the coffee cup. "You didn't hear it from me. Official records get lost or damaged all the time. Why, just last year there was that big flood, and the parish courthouse ain't all that watertight. But neither is Mrs. O'Halloran's inheritance without proof of her marriage."

"But Alphonse knows they were married—he was Jimmy's partner. And *you* know. You all can vouch for her, right?"

"I reckon that's why Alphonse and Kelly are on this train with her, and why they're worried about you talking to the law. They're afraid you know something they don't."

"Me? What would *I* know?" I said.

"Everyone knows something," Leon said, not all that helpfully.

"They ain't taking any risks," Clovis said. "They're counting on that money."

"I thought it was for Mrs. O'Halloran and her baby."

Clovis nodded. "Alphonse has agreed to vouch for the widow's marriage to Mr. O'Halloran, and she's agreed to give him full ownership of the club if the insurance comes through."

"How do you know that?" I demanded. I liked this Clovis fellow well enough, but I was starting to feel sore that everyone knew more than I did.

Clovis gave a little shrug, the kind that's more in the eyebrows than the shoulders. "I hear things working the clubs."

"Well what do you hear about Kelly and that other fellow? The real big one. Malcolm?"

"Malcolm Sloan is the bouncer at the Cajun Queen. He's

worked for Alphonse for years. As for Mr. Kelly . . ." Clovis paused, his expression shifting to disgust. He took a long sip of his coffee before he spoke again, as if trying to wash a bad taste from his mouth. "I ain't acquainted with Mr. Kelly, but there's something mighty unsettling in how he looks at Nettie sometimes."

"And what about you?" I asked.

"What about me?"

"Why are you going to Chicago?"

Clovis laughed. He had a deep, rippling laugh, warm and sturdy. "Music, my friend! The boys and me, we figure it's time to strike out. Jazz is hot these days, and not just in New Orleans. We're headed to Chicago to make the Clovis Dupré Orchestra the talk of the town all across America!"

"Without Nettie—I mean, Mrs. O'Halloran? Do you have someone else singing?"

"Nettie hasn't sung with us for a while. We're just instrumental now. Fact is, ain't nobody who can replace Nettie." A wistful look came across his face.

"Would you take Nettie back if she asked?"

Clovis's mouth fell open and his eyebrows popped up, but then he quickly regained his composure. "Back in the orchestra, you mean? Of course we would. With her voice, we could make a mint."

"Then she'll be okay, even if the insurance doesn't come through, right?"

Clovis smiled. "If only the world was that simple, son."

Somehow, I didn't mind that he called me son. It felt kind and honest, and it pulled at my heart just a little. I reckoned

Clovis was the sort of fellow anybody would be glad to have as family.

"Why isn't it that simple?" I asked.

"Well, in case you ain't noticed, Mrs. O'Halloran and me, we ain't sharing a car on this here train."

"But she sang with you before," I pointed out.

"That was before she became Mrs. O'Halloran," he said. Then he gave me a long look. "There's choices a person makes in life that you can't go back on once they're made." He drained his cup, set it on the table, and stood. "Now if you'll excuse me, the boys are waiting for me in a game of dominoes."

I watched him walk away. I didn't see why Nanette couldn't go back on the stage just because she'd been married to Jimmy O'Halloran. If I'd been Mrs. O'Halloran, looking for friends and a life for my baby in this hard world, I'd have taken this kind Dupré fellow over the slippery Cajun or the ice-hard Irishman any day.

"He didn't eat his corn bread," Terrance said, jarring me from my thoughts. "Can I have it?"

We split it down the middle.

GRENADA, MISSISSIPPI
2:52 P.M.

Leon pondered the whole time Terrance and I ate. "Something's mighty fishy here," he said. "If the insurance money is for the widow, why is Brian Kelly counting on it? And her arrangement with Alphonse Bujeau, what's that about? He'll vouch for Miss Nettie's marriage to Mr. O'Halloran so she can get the insurance money, but why would Miss Nettie ever give up her share of the Cajun Queen in return? It's got to be worth more than insurance, doesn't it?"

Terrance piped up. "If I owned something that nice, I wouldn't give it up for nothin'. No matter what it was worth!"

I chewed my corn bread, considering. "So it's fancy, then? You've been there, to the Cajun Queen?"

Terrance giggled. "Bobby Lee don't know nothing about the Cajun Queen," he told Leon, as if Leon couldn't see that for himself. "He didn't even know who Jimmy O'Halloran was before he got on the train and met up with his widow."

Leon smirked like an annoying know-it-all.

"Oh, and I suppose you fellows took tea with him every afternoon, did you?" I said, feeling more hot under the collar by the minute.

Terrance giggled even harder. "You're funny, Bobby Lee. It's easy! If you give a quarter to the stagehand, he'll prop the back door open and you can listen from the alley. So we take up a collection and then he lets us kids peek in, as long as we stay quiet, so that's how we know it's nice. Plenty of colored folks gather there when the best bands are playing. Ain't nothing better than good jazz at the Cajun Queen, even if it is from the alley."

"Is that how y'all met Clovis Dupré?"

"Everyone in the Eighth Ward knows Clovis," Terrance said.

"Everybody knows everybody in the Eighth Ward, period," Leon clarified. "Everyone takes care of their neighbors. Clovis has helped plenty of folks out of hard times with the money he makes playing jazz."

"Yeah, well," I said, feeling sore all over again, "if y'all know so much, and about so many people, then how'd Jimmy O'Halloran die?"

"That's easy," Leon said. "He fell from the third-story window."

"I know that! But what made him fall?" I asked. "Or who?"

Terrance's eyes opened wide. "You think it was on purpose?"

"You tell me," I said. "You're the experts."

"Well, I know what was in the papers, and what Clovis and the orchestra said after it happened," Leon said. "Rumors were running wild. There was a party upstairs in the Cajun Queen. A private party with all kinds of muckety-mucks who shouldn't oughta been at a gin joint."

"What's a gin joint?" Terrance interrupted him but Leon shushed him and went on with his story.

"Word spread about this big party upstairs, and pretty soon everybody and his brother was up to the third floor, trying to get past Malcolm Sloan and into that room. So Jimmy O'Halloran had to go try to clear them all out, but of course there was a scuffle. Folks started pushing and shoving, and next thing you know, ol' Jimmy goes right off the balcony and onto the pavement below. Broke his head clean open, they say. 'Course, when that happened, everybody ran outta the Cajun Queen like rats off a ship."

"What about the party?" I asked. Learning more about this private party on the night of Jimmy's death seemed like a good place to start if I really wanted to find out what happened.

"What about the party?" Leon asked.

"Who was at it? Why was it such a big secret?"

Leon shrugged. "How should I know? Probably the mayor, or the chief of police, or someone like that. Their type's always going to gin joints and trying to cover it up. Why do you want to know?"

"There's this cop back there," I said, gesturing in the direction of my train car.

"The one we saw in Jackson?"

"That's the one. Sergeant Hayworth. He says Mrs. O'Halloran's group is a bunch of cold-blooded murderers. He's following them all the way to Chicago, trying to get something on them."

"Nanette O'Halloran wouldn't have killed Jimmy!"

"I don't reckon so either. But I bet we could figure out who did, and why, if we knew what was going on that night at the Cajun Queen. If the mayor or the chief of police was there like you say, maybe Sergeant Hayworth is trying to hush something up. Or maybe it was some other kind of illegal dealings. It must have been something big if Bujeau and Jimmy were trying so hard to keep the party private."

"And big enough to get Jimmy killed!" Terrance said, his eyes big and bright with excitement.

"You know," Leon said slowly, "that Malcolm fellow would know what was going on there that night. Didn't Clovis say he was in the car back yonder with you?"

"You're right," I said. I turned to Terrance. "You told me you wanted to investigate about the man in the box. Do you still, now that you know who it is?"

"Boy, do I ever!" Terrance said.

"What exactly do you have in mind?" Leon asked.

"I'll talk to Malcolm to see what he knows, if you and Terrance will have a look in Bujeau, Kelly, and Mrs. O'Halloran's luggage in the baggage car."

"What are we looking for?" Terrance asked.

"For that insurance policy. To find out if she really has it on her. And for anything that might link Jimmy's death to what went on at that party that we don't know about. Secret dirty dealings that maybe the police didn't want anyone finding out about."

"I can't go through people's luggage!" Leon said.

"Are you chicken?" I taunted, glad to be getting a little of my own back.

"I ain't chicken, but I ain't stupid neither. What if I get caught?"

"Just tell 'em you were doing your job and the trunk popped open. You were just putting everything back that fell out."

"White folks won't believe that, even if they did bother to ask," Leon said. "If it looks to them like I'm stealing, then I'm stealing far as they're concerned, and it's off to jail I go. No slap on the wrist like you'd get."

"But if you were doing your job—" I tried again, a little humbled but still determined.

Terrance snorted. "Leon's got no job here."

"Hush up, Terrance!" Leon said, sharper than before.

I turned back to Leon, glowing in triumph. "I knew it!" I crowed. "So what *were* you doing with the mail earlier?"

"Our granddaddy works the train," Terrance offered, still as bright and cheerful as ever. "And our pop works the cotton. So during the planting and the picking, he's gotta go away and we's with Granddaddy."

"That still doesn't explain what you were doing with the mail," I said.

Leon ground his teeth. "I'm no freeloader!" he said, the heat of his embarrassment burning right through into his words.

"You won't tell, will you, Bobby Lee?" Terrance said, giving me those big, innocent doe eyes again.

"No," I said, although I wasn't really sure what there was to tell. I hadn't exactly gotten an answer to what Leon was doing working with the mail and baggage, except that it wasn't on the up-and-up.

But for now, I wanted to know about what had happened to Jimmy O'Halloran more than whatever Leon was up to, so I let it slide. Something had been going on in that third-floor room that had gotten Jimmy killed, I was sure of it, and while I didn't know what it was, I did know it smelled like opportunity. After all, if Bujeau was willing to pay me two hundred dollars to keep my mouth shut when I didn't actually know anything, who knows what he or Kelly would pay if I *did* know something? And if knowing could help me help Nanette O'Halloran, all the better.

But of course, knowing more meant convincing Leon to help. "You won't get caught, Leon," I coaxed. "No one caught you before when you were in the baggage car."

"*You* did," he pointed out.

"You want to find out what really happened that night, don't you?"

"Sure I do. But I got my family to consider. I got to watch out for Terrance, and I don't want to get my granddaddy in trouble."

"If Jimmy O'Halloran was murdered, there might be a big reward for catching his killer," I said. "A reward would be a big help to your family. And if we get one, I'll split it with you right down the middle."

Leon considered for a moment. "There's two of us and only one of you, so why should we split it down the middle? Besides, I'm the one taking all the risk. We split it three ways, or I'm not doing it."

I began to argue, since they were together and Terrance was too little to be much help. Then I remembered that there wasn't likely to be any reward anyway, since I had no intention of turning anyone over to Sergeant Hayworth. I smiled. "You drive a hard bargain, Leon. But okay. A three-way split."

We shook on it.

"Remember," I said. "You're looking for an insurance policy. And anything else that seems suspicious. Documents, money, smuggled goods. Anything that gives us a hint about what got Jimmy killed."

"And you'll talk to Malcolm?" Leon asked.

"Soon as I can get him alone." Not that I had any idea how to do that, but I'd try. A prickle of excitement flushed across my skin. This just had to be my big break!

"There'll be more mail to load at our next stop. I'll try then," Leon said. "Meet us back here after you talk to Malcolm and we'll share what we learn."

I agreed, barely even feeling guilty about taking advantage of them. It wouldn't be my fault if there was no reward, or if we didn't catch the killer, assuming there even was one. For all I knew, it really had been an accident. And Leon had proved himself pretty clever—I didn't figure he'd get caught. I was taking a risk too, talking to the muscle-bound bouncer. If he suspected me of sticking my finger between the tree and the bark, he'd squish it flat—it and all of the rest of me right along with it.

I walked back to my own car, wondering how I would get Malcolm alone. I was thinking, too, of the two hundred dollars Bujeau had offered me, before Dupré had interrupted us and the money had returned to his pocket. I hadn't told Terrance and Leon about that. It would be all mine, once I could get a chance to negotiate with Bujeau. And if I'd learned the secret of Jimmy's death before I negotiated . . . I wasn't sure how much money was in a roll that size, but I wouldn't mind finding out.

I returned to the whites-only car to find it surprisingly busy. Countrywomen had apparently been boarding at the last few stops while I was in the colored car. Judging from the baskets of eggs, live chickens, and other miscellany, they were local women who'd been out doing their marketing. One leathery old suntanned woman was chewing on a corncob pipe and scratching the ears of the piglet in her lap as if she was a hillbilly duchess and it was her toy poodle. All in all, they filled the car with enough noise and chaos that my return was hardly noticeable to anyone except for Brian Kelly, who watched my every move as I made my way down the aisle.

My small bag was still where I'd left it, holding my seat. On top of it I found a small, neatly folded slip of paper. I carefully unfolded the note and read the stiff, blunt handwriting inside:

There are things you should know. Meet me in the smoking lounge. It is in your best interest.

The note was unsigned, and of course I had no way of recognizing the handwriting, but I thought I knew who it was from. Bujeau and Malcolm were both absent from the car, but of the two, Bujeau didn't care one bit about my best interest. I folded it back up and smiled to myself. My luck was changing for sure.

I squared my shoulders, and even though I saw Kelly watching me with suspicion, made my way back, in search of the smoking lounge.

ONE HOUR FROM MEMPHIS, TENNESSEE
4:02 P.M.

The smoking lounge was at the very rear of the train and had a sign on the door that read GENTLEMEN ONLY. I knew I didn't meet that description. Then again, there were quite a few adult men who didn't either, and I doubted it kept them out, so I opened the door and stepped inside. A stinking blue haze hung in the air. Through it, I could see the rows of fine, velvet-upholstered chairs on either side of the aisle, many of them occupied by so-called gentlemen, puffing away at cigars and cigarettes. I looked around for a familiar face, but didn't see one. Instead, I saw a familiar back, almost too broad for the chair, which was turned so that he looked out the window. Malcolm. Exactly who I wanted to see.

Then I remembered that he wanted to see me, too—and this caused me to hesitate in the doorway a moment longer. He was bound to know what happened behind closed doors the night Jimmy O'Halloran died. But what did he want from me? Had Bujeau or Kelly ordered him to rough me up? I didn't want to get flattened.

Malcolm turned while I was still considering. "You've come this far, Bobby Lee," he called. "Sit down and hear me out. I won't lay a finger on you. I swear."

I crossed to the chair beside him, my nerves thrumming with excitement and fear. Malcolm took one long puff of his cigar, blew the smoke out of the corner of his mouth, and fixed me with a steady eye, sizing me up for a full minute before he spoke. I admit, I was surprised to see such a shrewd gaze from the hired muscle.

"Mr. Bujeau's planning to offer you that money again to favor his version of the story with Sergeant Hayworth. And it ain't my place to tell you whether or not to take it. I myself am on Mr. Bujeau's payroll, and I'll tell Hayworth exactly what Mr. Bujeau tells me to tell him. But you're just a kid. You need to know one thing before you take Bujeau's offer. Jimmy O'Halloran's death was no accident."

I tried to look cool and calm, even though my heart was hammering away a mile a minute. Getting the information I came for was going to be easy as pie. "How do you know?" I asked, trying not to sound too eager.

"There was an ironwork railing on the balcony outside that window. It should have kept Jimmy from falling, but the bolts had been removed from the railing. Someone *planned* for Jimmy to go through that window that night."

"Who would do such a thing?" I asked, mimicking Terrance's innocent, wide-eyed stare. "Do you think it was someone at the party?"

Malcolm's eyes narrowed with suspicion. "Who said anything about a party?"

"It was in the papers," I said quickly, seeing I'd hit a tender spot.

Malcolm took another puff of his cigar, eyeing me as he did

so. "Let me give you a piece of advice, young man. In this company, it ain't wise to be asking a lot of careless questions."

"Sorry, sir," I said, still going for guileless innocence. "I just feel mighty sorry for Mrs. O'Halloran and that sweet little baby of hers. That's all."

His eyes softened at the mention of Mrs. O'Halloran.

"You're fond of Miss Nettie?" he asked.

"Miss? Shouldn't that be Mrs.?"

"I've known her for a long time. She will always be Miss Nettie to me."

"A long time?" I said. I was trying to frame my next question, but it turned out I didn't need to. Not on this topic.

He smiled, his big face turning as sweet and tender as a baby's. "I've known Miss Nettie since before Jimmy O'Halloran ever brought his Irish luck to New Orleans. Since Mr. Bujeau owned a crummy little back-alley dive in Storyville and Miss Nettie was just a stick of a girl, singing on his stage."

"When was that?" I asked.

Malcolm took another long draw on his cigar and stretched out his legs. "1917," he said. "Sad times, what with the war. Miss Nettie, though, she was there every night, singing her heart out. She *had* to sing."

"For the money?"

"For her *soul*, you know? That's why when Clovis Dupré heard her, he asked her to join his group. She had angels and devils all twisting around together in that voice, and a fellow couldn't listen to her sing without getting all stirred up inside. With her singing, the Clovis Dupré Orchestra really took off. They were in demand, playing all over town."

"And that's how she met Jimmy O'Halloran?"

"Jimmy came to town looking for opportunity. He found Alphonse Bujeau and then he found Miss Nettie. When he saw her, he could think of nothing else. He had to have Nanette LeBlanc for himself. And for his club."

"Did he love her? Or did he just want her singing in his new place?" This wasn't the information I'd come for, but I couldn't help asking. There was something about the story that filled me up and left me wanting more.

"Love isn't a strong enough word for his passion. He was on fire for her, and in no time she was mad about him too. They were seen all over town with her on his arm, living high. Of course, the real upper crust couldn't condone them—a Yankee Irishman and a gal of her background. But it's the twenties now, and folks don't care so much about who you are as who you make yourself into. Jimmy was nothing if not a self-made man—and he made Nanette over right along with him. Bujeau too. By the time the Cajun Queen opened, everybody who was anybody couldn't wait to be seen there."

"But if it was a high-society supper club, how did they have the Clovis Dupré Orchestra playing for them?" I asked. "I thought colored folks could only play for colored folks."

Malcolm nodded. "That was a problem for them. See, in Chicago it ain't like that. But in New Orleans, Jimmy had to come up with a different way. He had been sneaking into the Negro clubs, scoping the talent, and he was convinced that a lot of the best bands were the colored bands."

"Like the Clovis Dupré Orchestra."

"That's right. So Jimmy, he put up a curtain across the stage, all spangled with glitter, and he put the orchestra behind it and Miss Nettie in front, a single bright spotlight turning her as pure and white as an angel in the heavens while all that dark, sultry jazz rose up around her out of nowhere.

"It was pure genius. And when she opened her mouth to sing, mm, mm, mm. *Enchanté,* as Mr. Bujeau would say."

"Did folks know the orchestra was colored?" I asked.

"Sure they did. That was one of the big attractions, white folks getting to listen to one of the really good colored bands without risking going to a colored club, and with that black curtain meeting the requirements of Jim Crow. After all, the laws weren't meant to keep white folks from getting their fair share of good music."

"So the club was a success and Jimmy and Nanette got married?" I asked.

"It was a success all right. Especially after Prohibition. The Cajun Queen had connections that kept the good times flowing, if you take my meaning."

"Connections?" I said, sitting up a little straighter. I'd been lulled by the love story and memories of good times, but I was alert again now. "Is that where Mr. Kelly comes in?"

Malcolm gave me a warning glance. "You're asking those careless questions again," he said. "You'd be wise to mind your own business where Kelly's concerned."

So Kelly *was* a criminal! Now I was getting somewhere. "What about Alphonse Bujeau?" I asked, risking one more careless question while he was in the mood to talk. "He had a place in New Orleans before Jimmy showed up. Surely he had connections too."

"Bujeau's better at spending money than at making it." Malcolm stood. "So think carefully before you make any deals with anyone, young man. There's more to this than meets the eye. Jimmy's connections may have cost him his life. And just because he's dead, don't mean those connections are severed."

"But that's what I wanted to ask you about. That's why I came here. To find out what was going on at the Cajun Queen that night."

Malcolm shook his head, slow and full of warning. "You don't need to know that, Bobby Lee. That question is more than careless. It's dangerous."

"Do the others know that he was murdered?" I asked.

Malcolm's mouth tightened. "Why do you think Mr. Bujeau is traveling with a bodyguard? Now if you'll excuse me, I've got to get back on duty."

He turned and walked away, leaving me to contemplate what had happened, and what might happen still.

HALF AN HOUR FROM MEMPHIS, TENNESSEE
4:30 P.M.

I gave Malcolm plenty of time to get away from the smoking lounge before venturing out myself. I hadn't learned who was at the party, thanks to having fallen once again, like a lovesick ninny, into Nanette's story. But I did know for sure now that Jimmy O'Halloran had been murdered, and that whoever Kelly was, he was someone to be feared—even by the likes of the gigantic, knuckle-cracking Malcolm Sloan. Did Nanette know he was dangerous? Did she know her husband had been murdered? Was she in danger too? If so, the sooner I found out what had happened to Jimmy and why, the sooner I could protect her.

I was eager to meet up with Terrance and Leon, to see what they'd learned, in the hopes we could put it all together and solve the mystery. But I didn't want to go rushing off, calling attention to myself—or to the fact I'd met with Malcolm.

So I sat in the plushy velvet chair in the smoking lounge and watched the Mississippi Delta roll by in the afternoon sun. Mile after mile of newly sprouted cotton seedlings spread their broad leaves to the sun. Here and there, families of sharecroppers worked the fields, kids pulling weeds while their parents hoed the rows. Mothers, their faces hidden in floppy sunbonnets, worked beside their husbands, their babies strapped to their backs. Whole families, blacks and whites alike, scraping along for an honest living under the blistering sun. I ran my hands over the velvet of the upholstery, enjoying its luxury all the more. I'd have a chair like this in every room of my mansion when I made it rich in Chicago.

I spent a half hour in comfort before I set out toward the front of the train in search of Terrance and Leon. Instead, halfway through the dining car, I came across Alphonse Bujeau. He was sitting with Malcolm at a table, eating pie and drinking coffee. He called my name and waved me toward an empty seat at his table. I glanced at Malcolm. His face was completely expressionless, giving away nothing of our conversation. He was back on the clock, on Bujeau's payroll.

Bujeau smiled and fingered his ruby-studded watch chain as I took the seat. I thought about what Malcolm had said, about Bujeau being better at spending money than making it. That watch chain was worth a pretty penny. So were the rings on the plump, sausagey fingers that fidgeted with it.

"I think you know why I want to talk to you, don't you, boy?" Bujeau said after we'd eyed each other for a moment.

"Not entirely, sir," I said, hoping that if I played dumb I might get answers out of him that I hadn't gotten out of Malcolm.

He smiled. "You like Nanette, don't you? You want to see her and her baby taken care of?"

"'Course I do."

"Then you'd want to side with me, and not go ratting to that cop. Right, kid?"

I glanced at Malcolm. His eyes were focused off in the distance, his face expressionless. I turned back to Bujeau.

"Well now," I said, "I can't promise to side with you when I don't rightly know what your side is."

"My side is, I'm trying to take care of Nanette. I'm trying to take care of my business. I don't need a meddling cop interfering with that."

"Seems to me your business should take care of Nanette. As Jimmy's widow, I reckon she's your partner in his place now." I watched him closely to see what his expression might give away, but he was too interested in his plate of pie for much else to register in his eyes.

"Like I said before, kid, she's got other resources, if everything works out according to plan. To that end, I'm offering you one hundred dollars when we get to Chicago, if you tell Hayworth what I tell you to tell him."

"I believe the deal was *two* hundred dollars. If I'm going to get involved, you're going to have to make it worth my while," I said, mimicking Kelly's chilly calm.

Bujeau slammed his fist on the table, making the china cups rattle against their saucers. The waiter scurried over.

"Is everything all right, sir?" he asked.

Bujeau relaxed his fist and waved the waiter away. "Okay, kid. Two hundred," he said when we were alone again. "But for two hundred, you'll do and say exactly what I tell you, *n'est-ce pas*? You work for me now. If anyone asks, Nanette and Jimmy married and had a baby, and Jimmy's death was a tragic accident."

This was what I wanted to hear! Two hundred dollars, and who knew what else when I figured out what had really happened. I might have a ruby watch chain and rings, and plump fingers of my own. Or better yet, a pin-striped suit and cool confidence like Kelly. With two hundred dollars, I could take my time finding my way into the Chicago crime rackets. Of course, if I impressed Kelly before I got to Chicago, I'd already have my in, and could go straight for the rubies.

I glanced again at Malcolm. He was still mostly expressionless, but I could see his jaw was clenched. Poor Malcolm. He'd taken the trouble of warning me, thinking I was an innocent kid. He was undoubtedly disappointed to discover the depths of my criminal soul. I looked back at Bujeau, meeting his glare without flinching.

"How do I know you'll pay me when we get to Chicago?" I asked.

"Under the circumstances, you are going to have to trust me, kid."

I shook my head. "I need to see some money on the barrelhead."

I expected Bujeau to slam his fist on the table again, but instead he gave me a crafty half smile. *"Chaque chien gratte pour son os,"* eh, kid?" he said, which meant: Every dog scratches for his bone.

I shrugged, still meeting his gaze. *"Chaque chien hale sa couene,"* I replied. Every dog has to carry his own hide.

Bujeau laughed and reached into the inside breast pocket of his suit. He pulled out a roll of bills and peeled off twenty dollars. "I think we'll make fine business partners, Mr. Claremont," he said, holding the money out to me. "The remainder will be paid when we get to Chicago. Don't disappoint me."

I took the money. "All I know is that Nanette and Jimmy married and had a baby, and Jimmy's death was a tragic accident." I got to my feet and tucked the twenty dollars into my pocket. "A pleasure doing business with you, Mr. Bujeau."

I turned then to walk away, but as I did I saw Malcolm's silent lips turn down, into a tight, disapproving frown.

MEMPHIS, TENNESSEE
5:02 P.M.

Despite Malcolm's scowl, I was flying high when I left Bujeau. Twenty dollars in my pocket and one hundred eighty more when we got to Chicago! And even though I hadn't learned who was at the party, I was getting a clearer understanding of things. Or at least, I was starting to form better questions.

Malcolm had said the Cajun Queen had connections that kept the good times flowing. Judging from the newspaper headline I had folded in my pocket, I was sure those good times were being produced in Chicago. And Jimmy O'Halloran was *from* Chicago. The way Malcolm had hedged when I asked about Bujeau's connections, I was sure Jimmy was the one at the Cajun Queen with connections to Chicago's bootleg industry.

It had to be more than a coincidence that Kelly had been visiting Jimmy from Chicago at the time of Jimmy's murder. And the way Malcolm had warned me about Kelly, Kelly *had* to be part of the bootlegger connection, didn't he? He was probably the one Jimmy was dealing *with*!

But did that mean he was also involved in Jimmy's death? What would he have to gain by Jimmy being dead?

Then again, maybe he wasn't involved at all. It was mighty suspicious that Bujeau had recruited me to tell Sergeant

Hayworth that Jimmy's death had been an accident. If someone else had killed his partner, it seemed to me Bujeau would want that someone caught.

As best I could figure, the only thing that ever stood between Bujeau and owning the entire Cajun Queen was Jimmy. Bujeau had told me he didn't *want* the Cajun Queen to himself, that Jimmy was the life of the place, but what if those were just pretty words? If Bujeau loved and spent money like Malcolm said, he might have *needed* Jimmy out of the way and the club's profits all to himself.

All to himself, that is, if Nanette got her insurance money and signed the club over to him. I was a little worried by what Bujeau had said—"if things went according to plan." Was there more to it than just convincing the insurance company Nanette and Jimmy were married?

I recalled how Sergeant Hayworth had tried to point a finger at Nanette too, when he and I first spoke. But even after all I'd learned, I was still sure she was innocent. She was just on the way to Chicago, looking for the best life possible for her son. I had a hard time believing she had anything to do with the schemes of her acquaintances.

Thinking on this, I felt a little guilty about taking twenty dollars from Bujeau, the man who might have killed the love of her life. So I vowed that once I knew what exactly had happened to Jimmy, I would use Bujeau's money not just for my benefit, but for Nanette's too. I could protect her, if I knew who to protect her from. And who knows, protecting her might be worth a chunk of change to Kelly or Bujeau too. Assuming one of them wasn't heading off to jail.

The conductor was walking through the cars to announce our approach to Memphis, only five minutes away, so I hurried forward to see what Leon and Terrance had learned in the baggage car. The colored lounge car was nearly empty. Folks had all gone back to their seats to get ready for the stop in Memphis, so I passed through to the passenger car beyond.

It was shabby and suffocating. My gut twisted as I breathed in the hot air smelling of unwashed bodies and coal smoke, which was being sucked in through the open windows since we were so close to the engine. How could folks ride all the way to Chicago like this, and why did they have to when there was space in the car I was in? Would it hurt anything if colored folks could get a decent seat on a train, I wondered with annoyance. I squinted, and craned my neck, but there was a sea of people crowded into the stiff wooden seats or standing in the aisles, and I couldn't see a couple of boys in all that. I stepped forward, intending to walk through to look for them, but an old man in a porter's uniform blocked my way. His dark face was lined with wrinkles, and his hair and eyebrows were pure white with age. He shuffled out of his booth and stood before me, trying to straighten his stooped spine enough to look imposing.

"Can I help you, sir? I think you might be looking for a car back yonder," he said, pointing a gnarled finger back the way I had come. Back toward the nicer part of the train where the white folks were. Where the seats were more comfortable and the engine's smoke and cinders weren't blowing in on the travelers.

"I'm looking for two boys I met earlier, Terrance and Leon. I think they'd be sitting up here," I said, still scanning the passengers for any sign of the boys.

The old porter's face registered worry, bordering on fear. "Did these boys cause you trouble, sir?"

I looked at him and realized he must be their granddaddy.

"No, not at all! They're friends of mine," I said.

"Friends?" His eyebrows raised. Why did it always have to raise suspicion, white kids and colored kids acting friendly?

I looked him square in the eye. "Yes, sir. I met them while I was eating lunch."

The porter frowned at me, but nodded once. "So you're the boy I been hearing about. If you will wait back yonder, I'll see what I can do," he said, pointing me back toward the lounge car. I was happy enough to go. Being conspicuous made me feel plenty nervous at the best of times, and being the only white face in the colored folks' less-than-equal car made me feel downright naked.

I didn't wait long before Leon and Terrance showed up.

"Well?" I said. "Did you find the insurance policy? Did you learn anything?"

"Shh!" Leon said, glancing around us. The lounge car was empty, except for one young fellow wiping down the counters. Leon leaned close to me, and Terrance followed suit. "Looks like they're all traveling light, 'cept Mrs. O'Halloran," Leon whispered. "She's the only one with any baggage in the baggage car. She's got a trunk and two suitcases."

"Because she's planning to move to Chicago for good," I said. "The others are just seeing her off. Did you look in her trunk?"

Leon nodded. "Nothing. Just a lot of fancy clothes and shoes and perfume."

"She's a proper lady!" Terrance said, smiling. "I never saw so many lacy underthings."

Leon blushed. "You were supposed to be keeping a lookout, not ogling her underthings," he said.

"What did *you* find, Bobby Lee?" Terrance asked.

"Jimmy O'Halloran was definitely murdered," I said, and I repeated what Malcolm told me about the bolts on the balcony.

"How'd Malcolm know?" Leon asked. "Do you think he did it?"

"I doubt it. Why would he tell me Jimmy was murdered if he was the one who did it?"

"So *Bujeau's* the killer, then?" Terrance asked.

"I'm not sure. Bujeau had a good reason to kill Jimmy—they owned the Cajun Queen Supper Club together, and he'd have had all the profits to himself without Jimmy, so long as he can get Nanette out of the way. Plus, he's nervous as a cat."

"That don't prove anything," Leon said. "I'd be nervous too. If he's not the killer, that still means someone killed his partner. That would make me downright jumpy."

I nodded. "Yeah. But still, it's plenty clear he's trying to hide something. He offered me money to be his stooge to the police. Look." I showed them the twenty dollars he'd given me. I knew it wasn't smart, but I couldn't resist. I'd never had so much money before. Obviously, from the looks on their faces, they hadn't either. Leon whistled. Terrance tried to whistle, but with the gap where his front teeth should be, it came out as a sloppy, wet sound that left little sprinkles of spit on the table.

"So you're working for a crook now," Leon said.

I admit, I liked the way that sounded. Working for a crook made me a crook too. "Maybe. Maybe not. There's that Brian Kelly fellow too. He's from Chicago, and Jimmy's connections for booze had to be in Chicago."

"You mean, gangsters?"

I nodded again. "If O'Halloran was dealing with the Chicago mob, Kelly might not be a friend at all. He might have been sent to New Orleans to kill Jimmy."

"But why?" Terrance asked.

I shrugged. "I don't know that the Chicago mob needs much of a reason, but so far, I don't know that they had any reason at all."

The train whistle blew, to indicate our approach to the station.

"Well," Leon said, grinning, "We'll find out soon. I bet the murder weapon is in either Bujeau's or Kelly's suitcase."

"There's no murder weapon—he fell out a window," I said.

"That was just a matter of convenience. If Kelly came down to Louisiana to kill Jimmy, he'll have a murder weapon," Leon said.

"Gangsters don't go nowhere without their heaters!" Terrance said, suddenly an expert.

I wasn't so sure about their logic. I didn't much figure a gun in someone's suitcase was going to prove anything. And anyway, they hadn't found anything like that in the baggage car, so I didn't see the point.

"We're coming into Memphis, you know," Leon said. "The

train'll change cars there, so it's a long stop. Most folks'll be getting off for lunch and to stretch their legs. It's a perfect chance for you to go through the bags they got with them at their seats."

I stared at Leon in disbelief. "I can't do that! What if I get caught?"

"Be the same as if we got caught," Leon said, giving me the eye. "And Terrance and me can't do it. We ain't allowed in the whites-only car. Are you chicken, Bobby Lee?"

"I ain't chicken," I said, knowing I'd been caught in my own device. "But what about the car's porter? Does he leave the carriage unattended?"

"We can distract him," Terrance said. "Chelton's a friend of Granddaddy's."

"Okay, I'll check their things, but you two have to keep an eye out. If Kelly is a gangster, he'll kill us if he catches us."

"Gangsters don't scare me!" Terrance said, sitting up straight and squaring his skinny shoulders, which just made him look even smaller in his oversized shirt.

"You ever met a gangster?" I asked him, trying hard to keep a straight face.

"No," he said. "But I ain't scared of nobody!"

"You are so," Leon said. "You're scared of the dark. And spiders. And ghosts."

Terrance's shoulders slumped a little, but his fierce expression didn't falter. "Those ain't people!" he said. "*People* don't scare me!"

"Well, you might want to be afraid of Kelly and Bujeau," I said. "If they'd kill a fella with a wife and baby, I doubt they'd be all that worried about killing any of us."

"Which one was Kelly, anyway?" Terrance asked.

"The Yankee who talked down to Clovis," Leon said, his teeth clenching as he thought about it. "Listen, Bobby Lee. We'll make sure Chelton's distracted, then we'll stand around by the train and make sure the others don't get back on early. If one of them comes along, we'll give you a signal and then stall them as long as we can."

"What kind of signal?" I asked.

"I can hoot like an owl," Terrance suggested.

I rolled my eyes. "You can't stand around in the Memphis depot hooting. Folks'll think you're a lunatic!"

The brakes screeched and we all rocked forward in our seats as we came into the station.

"Get on back there to your seat and open the window," Leon said. "Then we'll stand near it to keep watch, and if one of them comes back before you're done, we'll bang on the side of the train car. Understand?"

"Sure," I agreed.

"And once we roll out of Memphis, come on up here, nice and casual like, and tell us what you've found."

I agreed and hurried back to my car on the train, just as the brakes let out a last big puff of steam and she came to rest. Some folks bundled up their packages and hurried away with purpose, others left their things behind and strolled away at a more leisurely pace.

Sergeant Hayworth was one of the leisurely strollers. His hands were stuffed into his pockets and he was whistling as he walked up the aisle to the forward door. He gave me a little smile and nod as he passed. I nodded back, trying to look innocent. I took my time opening the window and collecting my belongings while Nanette and her companions gathered up their things. I wanted to make sure they were all long gone before I started pawing through their luggage.

Nanette O'Halloran took the baby from his basket and Mr. Kelly offered to carry some of the baby's things. I watched him closely as he did. He exhibited none of the tenderness of a true lover, nor the smooth flattery of a hopeful suitor. If he was after a prize, it wasn't her affection.

When she had the baby on her shoulder, the group left the car together. I stepped off too, from the front entrance, while they took the back. I'd planned to just loiter near the train until I was sure they were gone, then slip back on. But as soon as Mrs. O'Halloran and Mr. Kelly moved off through the crowd, Alphonse Bujeau waved me to him.

"This is where you start earning your pay, Mr. Claremont," he said. He pointed toward the retreating figures of Mr. Kelly and Mrs. O'Halloran. "Follow those two. I want to know everything Kelly is saying to her, got it?"

"I thought you were paying me to tell your story to the cops."

"I'm paying you to do as I say," Bujeau said. "Two hundred is a lot of cash. It's time for you to earn it."

I hesitated, but couldn't think of any way to say no. So, with a meaningful glance and shrug toward Leon, who was hovering near the baggage car, helping with the luggage and keeping an eye on me, I set out to tail Mr. Kelly and Mrs. O'Halloran. They had already disappeared off the platform and into the crowded station, so I had to hurry.

Unlike the rustic clapboard depots in the small towns we'd

passed through, Memphis had a large, modern station, all brick and echoing tile on the inside. A swarm of white folks moved through the whites-only waiting room, past its rows of wooden benches, toward the triple doors that opened out onto the street. I joined the crowd, glad for Mrs. O'Halloran's distinctive widow's weeds that made her stand out.

Outside, the street was busy. Cars and buggies were picking up and dropping off passengers and luggage. Dozens of pedestrians waited on the corner as a streetcar clanged by, then surged across the road to a row of shops and restaurants on the other side. Mrs. O'Halloran and Mr. Kelly were already crossing the street when I stepped out.

I waited on my side of the street. Mr. Bujeau had wanted me to find out what Mr. Kelly was saying to her, but I didn't see how I could get close enough to listen without being seen. And if I was seen, they certainly wouldn't say anything secretive.

Traffic whizzed by on the street while a new crowd of people pooled on the corner. I waited and watched my quarry stroll slowly along the sidewalk opposite, gazing in windows as they went. At last, traffic cleared and the mass of people spilled off the curb and across the street. For a moment, I lost sight of the couple, but the crowd dispersed when we reached the sidewalk and I spotted them.

I set off in their direction, examining things in windows as they were doing, trying to move gradually closer to them in a way they wouldn't notice. I glanced in their direction from time to time, checking whether I'd been seen. When it appeared I hadn't, I worked closer still, close enough to hear them if they had been talking. They seemed, however, to have nothing to say. Mrs. O'Halloran, the baby turned up over her shoulder, was looking at hats and gloves and other fine things in the windows, and Mr. Kelly was looking bored.

I was outside a candy store, two shops down from them, when I accidentally made eye contact with the baby. He cooed and wriggled in his mother's grasp. Then he let out a happy screech. I darted into the candy store as Nanette and Kelly both turned to look. I had been lucky it was a candy store and not a china shop. It looked natural for a kid to go into a candy store, so even if they saw me, they wouldn't necessarily think I was following them. At least, I hoped they wouldn't.

Normally, I wouldn't have wasted my money on something as useless as candy, but I was there now, and might need to prove I had gone in for a purpose. Besides, with my newfound wealth, I could splurge a little on a treat. So I went to the counter and asked for three scoops of the penny candy from the jars—one for me, one for Leon, and one for Terrace. The bored clerk took his time getting out the little paper bag and filling it for me. Then he was even slower making change for my dime. By the time I could return to the window at the front of the store and look out, Mrs. O'Halloran and Mr. Kelly had disappeared.

Cautiously, I stepped outside, looking in both directions. Nothing. Apparently they had stepped into a store as well. I started walking once again. I figured I could just keep glancing in windows until I spotted them. I passed a shoe store and a millinery shop, where I felt foolish looking in the window at the ladies' hats and gloves. No sign of them. Ahead of me, across an alley, there was a five-and-dime store, which seemed like a likely place to find them. Feeling hopeful, I picked up my pace as

I crossed the alley. I was halfway across when someone grabbed the collar of my jacket from behind, yanking me roughly into the alley and behind a row of trash cans. Before I could utter more than a yelp of surprise, I was thrown up against the brick wall. My head slammed against it hard. The breath left my lungs, my ears rang, and the edges of my vision filled with sparks.

Hands gripped the lapels of my shirt and gave me a shake, and Brian Kelly's face came into focus. A cigarette dangled between his lips, and he leaned in so close to me I could feel the heat of it on my face.

"What do you think you're doing, kid? Huh? Just what do you think you're doing?"

I couldn't form a single word. My head was throbbing.

"Answer me!" He gave me a hard shake and my head banged against the wall again.

"Nothing," I managed to choke out.

He gave a grunt of disbelief, spewing cigarette smoke into my face. Then he released my collar with one hand and began to pat along my body with it. In my jacket pocket he found the silver cigarette case I'd helped myself to earlier.

"Nothing, huh? Looks like I've caught me a pickpocket."

"I gotta make my way in the world somehow," I said, hopeful that if he thought I was a harmless pickpocket he'd let me off the hook. Or better yet, praise my criminal skills.

He reached back into the same pocket and pulled out the scrap of newspaper I'd carried with me from home. Cold amusement curled the corner of his lip, making the cigarette tip rise. "What's this? You keeping track of business in Chicago?"

"Ain't much money in picking pockets," I said, trying to sound cool and collected, despite being pinned to a wall by his meaty fist. Cool in the face of adversity was an important skill, and it had occurred to me this might be my job interview. "I'm looking for some new opportunities."

"Is that right?" he said, dropping the newspaper and going back to searching my clothes for something more interesting. His eyebrows rose when he heard the twenty-dollar bill crinkle.

"Well, well," he said, pulling it from my pocket and waving it in front of my face. "And what opportunity was this?"

I shrugged.

In return he gave me another hard shake, another bang on the head. The goose egg that had been forming there split and a warm trickle of blood seeped along my scalp toward my neck. "Who gave this to you? The cop?"

I shook my aching head. "Bujeau."

"Bujeau? Why?"

"You were there when he made the offer," I said.

"Yeah, not to talk to the cop. So why are you following me?"

The jig was up. I could see that lying to him would only get me roughed up worse. "I—I don't know. He didn't say. But if there's any—"

Kelly gave me one more hard shake. This time he released my collar, and when I banged against the wall, I slid down it, leaving a trail of blood and hair along the rough brick. I sat still, dazed and aching, my legs sprawled out before me on the dirty pavement. Kelly towered over me. He pocketed my twenty dollars, but under the circumstances, I decided not to protest.

"So Bujeau's bought you to do his business, has he," he growled. "Well, tell Bujeau that I'll take care of Nanette. He doesn't need to worry about her. He'd better start worrying about saving his own worthless hide instead. You tell him that for me."

He took one last long drag from his cigarette, then he dropped it between my sprawled feet and crushed it out with his foot. "And one more thing, kid. You might start thinking the same thing for yourself."

Without warning, he swung his foot, catching me square between the legs. I crumpled over in pain as he strode away.

As I lay behind the trash cans, I heard the bell jingle on the five-and-dime door, then Nanette's voice.

"Sorry that took me so long. What were you doing in the alley?"

"Just having a smoke and watching a rat in the trash," he said.

"Did Bobby Lee ever come along from that candy store?"

"Naw. He must not have seen us."

"That's a shame. I would have liked to treat him to something at the soda fountain. He's been so kind," Nanette said in her gentle voice.

"You know kids. He's probably making himself sick on sweets. Shall we get back to the train?" Kelly said.

Their footsteps faded away as I lay there in the alley, wishing I were dead.

MEMPHIS, TENNESSEE
5:55 P.M.

My mind floated in and out of a bloody haze for some time, until the sound of the train whistle pulled me back into the world. The whistle meant she'd be pulling out soon, with or without me. At the moment, without me wasn't sounding half bad. I didn't know how I would explain to anyone what had happened, and I didn't know that I wanted to either. Right now, the farther I was from Kelly the better. But Nanette was with him—and he had said he would "take care" of her. What did that mean? Was she in danger after all? If she was, who would warn her of Kelly? And, there was the matter of the money. One hundred eighty dollars waited only fifteen hours away, and after this, I figured I had earned it.

I pulled myself unsteadily to my feet, holding on to the wall and a trash can for support until my nausea and dizziness subsided. I tested my legs and found I could walk, or at least stagger, so I clenched my teeth against the pain and set off for the station, slightly hunched over.

As I went, I cursed my stupidity. I had grown up on the streets of the French Quarter—I knew better than to step into an alley without looking for thieves or pickpockets first! It was the oldest trick in the book when it came to shakedowns. I had warned Terrance and Leon that Kelly might be dangerous, but hadn't taken that warning to heart myself. Of course, if Kelly was a gangster, he wouldn't take kindly to being followed. What had I been thinking?

I thought again of his words—*I'll take care of Nanette.* My pace quickened. She thought he was a friend of Jimmy's. She trusted him. I pictured her being smashed up against a wall in a filthy ally, little Jimmy Jr. crying frantically where she had dropped him.

The train whistle blew again. I broke into a run, a shot of pain jarring through me each time my foot hit the pavement. Inside the station, my eyes jumped to the huge clock on the wall over the timetable. The train was due to leave any second. I put on one more burst of speed, dodging through the crowd toward the platforms.

All the doors on the train except one were closed when I arrived on the platform. The conductor was leaning out the doorway to my car with a worried expression. It changed to annoyance when he saw me and waved me forward frantically. The train's brakes released with a loud hiss of steam and she began to ease forward, even as I pulled myself up onto the step.

"Don't be getting off the train if you can't keep track of the time," the conductor scolded as he closed and sealed the door, not looking at me long enough to note my condition. "The Illinois Central doesn't wait for anyone."

I didn't respond. I only staggered to the nearest seat and dropped into it, my vision swimming. Then I let go and let everything go black.

DYERSBURG, TENNESSEE
6:36 P.M.

I woke to the concerned face of Nanette O'Halloran and the feeling of a cold towel being pressed painfully against the lump on the back of my head. The other occupants of the car were gathered behind Nanette, watching me with varying degrees of interest. I tried to sit up straighter and winced at the shock of pain between my legs. Nanette, seeing my expression, gently pressed me back down into a reclining position.

"Be still, Bobby Lee, you've taken a nasty knock on the head." I was glad she thought it was only my head that hurt. "I think you need a doctor."

"There must be a doctor somewhere on the train," Bujeau said, but no one moved to go find one.

I groaned. "I'll be fine. It's just a bump on the head is all. I've had worse."

"But you're bleeding," Nanette protested. "What on earth happened?"

I was looking past Nanette, at Bujeau and Kelly, standing side by side as if they were friends and not rivals. Kelly didn't seem all that concerned that I might rat him out, but Bujeau did.

"I was waylaid in an alley," I said. "It was stupid. I should have been paying more attention."

A slight smirk curled Kelly's lips, but he said nothing. Bujeau frowned.

"Good gracious!" Nanette said. "Were you robbed?"

I shrugged, or tried to. My head was pounding and any movement hurt. I couldn't exactly admit to losing possessions I shouldn't have had to start with, especially not to Nanette, who'd called me a good boy. "I didn't have anything to steal," I said.

"Did you see who did it?"

I glanced at Kelly, and winced at the gloating expression on his face. "It was just local kids, I think."

Nanette turned to Sergeant Hayworth. "You're a police officer. Aren't you going to do anything?"

"Well, unfortunately, the perpetrators are back in Memphis, and we're not, ma'am. There's not much I can do. But if young Mr. Claremont cares to make a statement, I can wire it back to Memphis at the next stop."

"I don't feel like talking just now," I said, closing my eyes. I couldn't bear to look at Kelly and Bujeau any longer. My embarrassment and shame at having been so foolish was making it hard for me to face them. I thought that if I pretended to need rest, they might leave me alone.

"He shouldn't go to sleep," Malcolm said. "He's likely concussed. He should stay awake until we're sure he isn't going into shock."

"Someone should sit with him," Nanette said.

"I'll stay with him for a bit," Sergeant Hayworth said. "That way if he wants to make a statement when he feels up to it, he can."

The others all agreed to this plan and dispersed, though Kelly gave me one last, challenging smirk, as if to say *Talk to the cop and you're dead, kid*. Not that he needed to; I wasn't a snitch. Unfortunately, I wasn't much of a criminal either, by the looks of it. I had proven myself too careless and naïve. And I hadn't warned Nanette either. All in all, I'd turned out to be useless. My only chance of saving face now was to keep my mouth shut and avoid giving Hayworth anything to chew on.

So I stretched out across the seat, letting my feet hang out into the aisle, gingerly positioning my bruised scalp against the cool towel that Nanette had left with me, intent on ignoring Hayworth. He took the seat opposite, facing me.

Hayworth didn't speak right away either. He leaned back in the seat and crossed his legs comfortably, watching me with a casual smile. The blissful silence lasted until the train made a brief stop in Dyersburg. But when the thin stream of local travelers had made their way on and off and the train rolled out of the station again, Hayworth spoke.

"What I'm trying to figure out," he said, "is how a kid who grew up on the streets of the Old Quarter could have gotten himself waylaid in an alley in Memphis."

I had been letting the rocking train lull me, but his words jarred me back awake. I swallowed hard, but I didn't look at him. I didn't want him to see my alarm, in case he was just making a guess about my past. After all, he could have guessed the Old Quarter had been my home from my accent, and my command of French.

"The Old Quarter's not such a bad place," I said cautiously. "Not all of it."

"But the parts you're familiar with are, aren't they, Robert E. Lee Claremont? With such a distinctive name it wasn't hard at all for me to make inquiries, which I did by telegraph back in Jackson. A detailed reply was waiting for me in Memphis. Seems there's a Sister Mary Magdalene back home who's mighty worried about your whereabouts. And there's the matter of twelve dollars missing from the fund for the poor at the Sisters of Charitable Mercy Convent."

I closed my eyes and let out a deep sigh. Why had I been so foolish as to tell a cop my real name? I had done nothing but make foolish mistakes since the moment I had left New Orleans. Now I would never see Chicago, or the rest of the two hundred dollars, for which I had just taken a beating.

I opened my eyes again and sat up. "Are you going to arrest me?"

"Well now, it seems that the Sisters really are feeling right charitable these days. Sister Mary Magdalene is willing to forgive the theft from the poor box if she can get you back, safe and sound." He gave a little chuckle. "Of course, they may have their own punishment worked out for you. You might prefer to go to jail."

I reckoned he was right about that. "Then you're sending me back?"

"You seem like a smart, capable young man, Bobby Lee, plenty capable to strike out on your own in the world. Hardly seems fair that you should be pinned down under the thumb of that old biddy at the convent."

I was a little surprised when a bolt of lightning didn't strike him down for calling Sister Mary Magdalene an old biddy. Sometimes it was hard to separate her in my mind from the vengeance of God himself. But as nothing fatal happened, I thought about what he had said, trying to make sense of it. If he wasn't going to arrest me or take me back to the Sisters, why had he bothered to find out about me, or tell me that he had? I waited, warily.

"Tell me, son. What have Bujeau and Mrs. O'Halloran been telling you? Because I know they've been talking, and I know they are up to something. A sweet-faced kid like yourself is apparently irresistible to the likes of them."

I shrugged. "Mrs. O'Halloran just told me about her husband and the first time they met."

"And Bujeau?"

"Nothing."

"And Mr. Kelly?"

I shook my head, then regretted it. "Not a thing."

"Tell me who beat you up, Bobby Lee."

"I already did. Just local nobodies."

Sergeant Hayworth gave an annoyed little sigh. "Maybe I haven't made myself clear. I know where you came from, and I know what you did. I could send you back. Or I could have you arrested and sent to the workhouse for delinquent children. Or . . ." He paused, to make sure he had my full attention. He did. "You can help me with my case and I'll help you with yours. You tell me what that crowd is up to, and I'll let you walk away in Chicago, free and clear. The nuns will never know I saw you or heard about the poor-box robbery."

"But I really don't know anything," I protested.

"Then find out," Hayworth said. "Unless you like the appeal of the workhouse."

I swallowed hard. I had agreed to tell the cop nothing, for two hundred dollars. But if I didn't tell him something, Bujeau's money would do me no good. On the other hand, if I went back on my word to Bujeau, who knew what he'd do to me. My future life of crime would end before it started if I caved in under pressure now. Just my luck. On a train full of criminals and murderers, the biggest snake was the cop who'd offered to protect me. If that wasn't proof of the merits of crime, I didn't know what was.

"What do you want me to find out?" I asked, my voice cracking a little with the shame of it.

"Bujeau and LeBlanc, or O'Halloran as she's calling herself. I want to know what they're up to. What kind of con are they planning to pull on Jimmy's relations in Chicago? Were they lovers before Jimmy O'Halloran died? I want you to learn everything about them that you can, and I want you to tell me."

"I don't think they trust me that much, Sergeant. They've all seen me talking to you."

"Well, make them trust you. Unless you're anxious to see the Sisters again, or to be working for the state of Louisiana." He patted my knee gently, as if he actually cared about my well-being. "I know it's hard to think now with your head aching as it does. We'll talk again further down the line, and you'll let me know what you've decided."

He stood and walked away, apparently no longer concerned for my health. Alphonse Bujeau, accompanied by the silent Malcolm, soon took his place. Unlike the sergeant, Bujeau made no attempt to pretend sympathy or kindness regarding my condition. He was angry. He leaned in close to me and hissed, "I expect the people I hire to do what they are paid to do."

"I did! I followed Mrs. O'Halloran and Mr. Kelly, like you told me to."

"And you let yourself get caught. I would have thought a guttersnipe from the Old Quarter would have better sense. Serves you right, getting kicked in the *bibittes*."

I winced again, both at his Cajun slang and at its truth. "How do you know that's what happened?" I said, wondering what Kelly had told him. I wondered, too, that he knew my background so well. Was I that transparent to everyone on the train?

When Bujeau answered me, it was entirely in Cajun French. "Because that's what he does, as a warning. I hope you learned something from him before you let him catch you."

"They weren't—"

"En français," he interrupted, glancing nervously past me toward where the others sat, apparently too close for comfort. *"Monsieur Kelly ne parle pas français."*

I began again in French. "They weren't plotting, if that's what you expected. They weren't talking about anything. They were only looking in shopwindows. Then Mrs. O'Halloran went into the five-and-dime, and he waited outside. That's when he caught me and told me to tell you he'd take care of Nanette from now on, and you should be thinking about saving your own skin."

"You told him I sent you?" Bujeau let out a string of Cajun curses that could have scorched the eyebrows off Beelzebub himself. "And what did Nanette say when she came out and saw he had given you a beating?"

"She didn't see. He left me in an alley, behind some trash cans. She asked what he had been doing and he only said he had been having a smoke. Mr. Bujeau, what did he mean about saving your skin?"

"What do you *think* he means, kid? You know what happened to my partner."

A chill went through me. Had Kelly killed Jimmy? Or did Bujeau kill him and Kelly was threatening to turn him in to the police? I leaned in closer to Bujeau and spoke quietly.

"Don't worry, Mr. Bujeau, I intend to earn that two hundred dollars. I won't let you down. It's just that it would be easier for me to learn what you want to know if I knew what information you're after. What do you think the two of them are up to?" I asked, still in French. I could see no point in taking unnecessary risks.

Bujeau glared at me. "I'm not paying you to stick your nose in *my* business. You do what I tell you, no questions asked. Keep your mouth shut and your ears open and report it all to me, understand? I will decide what's important and what isn't."

Bujeau stood and turned to Malcolm, speaking once again in English. "Stay with the brat and make sure he stays awake."

Malcolm gave one silent nod and Bujeau walked away. I let out a sigh and waited for Malcolm to take his turn at me, but he didn't. He remained silent, his expression impassive. I was grateful. I knew he could have said "I told you so," but he didn't. Bujeau had done me one favor. He had left Malcolm to watch me, and his presence would keep others away and give me time to think, as best I could with my aching head.

I hadn't realized that Kelly and Bujeau were so much at odds when I'd taken Bujeau's offer. If I wanted to get myself in with the Chicago rackets, it seemed I had taken a job with the wrong side. The question now was what to do about it. I didn't want to back out on Bujeau. For one thing, it was the only money I'd been offered. For another, Bujeau was likely to have Malcolm pound me flat if I became a turncoat after agreeing to work for him. And what if Kelly did mean to hurt Nanette? How could I work for him? Then again, if I thwarted Kelly by working with Bujeau, I'd never make it in the crime rings of Chicago. And then there was the whole mess with Hayworth.

I was caught between the tree and the bark, just as Bujeau had said. If I did what Bujeau was paying me to do, keeping silent with the cop, Sergeant Hayworth would force me back to New Orleans and maybe even have me busting rocks on a chain gang. But if I squealed to the sergeant, I wouldn't collect on the two hundred dollars, and I'd ruin my chance for a criminal career forever. I'd have to earn an honest living, which was another way to say a life of hard work and poverty. Plus, I'd have a reputation as a snitch, and Kelly would know it. That alone could get me killed in Chicago, a town where gangsters dined with the mayor.

I sighed and closed my eyes. Malcolm dutifully nudged my foot with his and I opened them again. "I wasn't sleeping," I said.

Malcolm said nothing.

I glanced past him to the front doorway that led to the colored cars up ahead. A movement there caught my eye. I watched, and a moment later Leon's face appeared in the window. I remembered then my promise to snoop through the baggage, which I hadn't kept. Another failing I'd have to own up to. Leon was gesturing with his hand, waving me toward him. I glanced back at Malcolm and tried to smile.

"I'm perfectly all right. You don't need to babysit me anymore."

Malcolm did not so much as blink in response. He took his instructions only from Mr. Bujeau.

I looked back at Leon and gave a little shake of my head. He gestured to me again, looking annoyed. I sighed and turned my face to the window. Even if Malcolm would let me, I couldn't risk going to talk to Leon and Terrance. Not with Hayworth, Bujeau, and Kelly all watching my every move.

I was still pondering my options, none of which seemed all that good, when the whistle blew and the train began to slow, signaling a stop ahead. A few minutes later, the conductor announced Fulton, Kentucky, with a transfer for all those headed for Louisville.

Louisville, Kentucky! That was the solution to all my problems! I had no idea what was in Louisville, but I knew what wouldn't be there—Alphonse Bujeau, Brian Kelly, or Sergeant Hayworth. I had no money, but I could probably get the ticket master at Fulton to exchange the remainder of my ticket to Chicago for one to Louisville. I would explain to him, weepy-eyed, that I had bought the wrong ticket, and my aunt was waiting for me in Louisville, and I was lost and all alone. Displays of frantic emotion were easy enough to conjure up, and usually got results.

I was sure that Sergeant Hayworth was more interested in catching Jimmy's murderer than in catching me. By the time he realized I'd given him the slip, he'd be headed for Chicago, and I doubted he'd bother to send anyone after me. But just in case, I'd play it smart this time. I'd get a ticket all the way to Louisville, but I'd get off someplace sooner, so he couldn't catch me at the end of the line. He wouldn't expect that. Not after all the simpleminded mistakes I had made so far. I'd be giving up the two hundred dollars from Bujeau, which I regretted, but under the circumstances there was no long-term future for me in Chicago, and far too much risk. Chances were, with Kelly's disapproval and Hayworth's threat, even if I went on to Chicago I'd have little chance to either collect or use the money.

I cheered up, even as the whistle blew and sent a spike of pain through my bruised head. My salvation was at hand, and my hopes for a future in crime restored. After all, Kentucky produced its fair share of moonshine.

FULTON, KENTUCKY
7:33 P.M.

"Watch your time, young man, and don't go getting yourself into more trouble, you hear?" the conductor said as I stepped down onto the platform at Fulton.

"Yes, sir," I said meekly. I gestured to my small bag of possessions, slung over my shoulder. "I'm just going to get cleaned up a little and come right back."

The conductor nodded grudgingly. Of course he wanted me to stay on the train, but he couldn't object to me washing the bloody grime off my face and neck either. Besides, I didn't care what he thought. It was the last time I'd ever see him.

I stretched as I stepped down onto the platform. It was evening and the first few breaths of cool air felt good on my sweaty skin. Unlike Memphis, Fulton was a small town, with a small, tidy depot, making it harder for me to disappear into a crowd. Colored ladies in pressed white uniforms stood with sandwich carts on the platform, ready to do a supper business, and I approached one, as an excuse to delay until more people had stepped down from the train and I could more easily blend in among them. Although neither the cop nor any of Mrs. O'Halloran's companions had made any move to get off the train, I knew I was being watched.

I paid a nickel for a ham sandwich and a glass of cold milk. That left me with only twelve cents from my windfall back in Jackson—enough to get me on to Louisville, where I'd find other sources of income. I drank the milk all at once and handed the glass back to the sandwich-cart lady, then I strolled causally into the station, nibbling the sandwich and mingling with the crowd.

Inside the station a corridor led two directions, with a sign pointing toward separate waiting rooms for colored and white folks. I headed toward the whites-only area. The room was clean and painted a cheerful bright yellow. One wall was taken up by a ticket booth, the opposite wall by the bathrooms. A line sprawled out from the ticket windows. I didn't see how I could stand in that line to exchange my ticket without being seen. Of course, there was a chance no one would come looking, but I wasn't going to take any more chances if I could help it. I looked up at the big timetable on the wall. The train to Louisville departed seven minutes after the train to Chicago. I could wait until the Chicago train was gone and then get my ticket for Louisville. All I had to do was find a place to hide myself from anybody who might drag me back onto the Chicago train before its departure.

I went to the bathroom and washed up, as I said I would. It felt good to get rid of the grime of my embarrassing encounter in Memphis. But the bathroom was too busy to be a hiding place. I couldn't stay there for the next half hour.

I stepped out of the bathroom and nearly collided with Leon. He had a suitcase in either hand and was walking about five steps behind a well-dressed white lady en route for the street.

"Leon," I said in surprise. "What are you doing here?"

He glanced at the woman, then slowed his step. "Meet me over yonder behind those trolleys in five minutes," he whispered, then hurried to catch up to the woman before she noticed his delay.

I looked in the direction he'd indicated. There was a phone booth on the wall beside the exit to the street. Next to it, a supply of baggage trolleys had been pushed into the corner. I walked toward them. Halfway across the room, I noticed Terrance peeking around the corner of the trolleys, gesturing wildly to get my attention. I glanced around. I could see no sign of Kelly, Bujeau, or anyone else keeping an eye on me, so I hurried to him. He crawled backward and I followed, to find myself in a cozy little corner, hidden from view by the phone booth on one side and the trolleys across the front.

"Won't you get in trouble for being in here?" I asked Terrance, glancing out at all the white folks.

"Naw. Leon and me carry people's bags for tips, so they lets us stay. White folks don't mind colored folks, long as we're working for 'em."

I glanced around one more time before I sat down beside him. I didn't want Kelly or Bujeau to find out Terrance and Leon were helping me, but now it was more for the brothers' safety than anything else. I figured it was safe to talk to Terrance there, though, where no one could see us. I would warn them to stay clear of Kelly, then we could go our separate ways. They could get back on the train for Chicago and I would wait there till it was gone and then get my ticket for Louisville. It was perfect.

"You don't look so good, Bobby Lee," Terrance said, giving me the once-over. "You fall off the train or something?"

"I got attacked, by Brian Kelly. He's definitely dangerous, Terrance. That's what I wanted to tell you and Leon."

"I know!" Terrance said, his eyes all lit up with excitement, like it was still all a game. "Just wait till we tell you what we found in—"

"Listen, Terrance," I said. "Y'all have to stay away from him, you hear? You don't want to end up like Jimmy O'Halloran, do you?"

Terrance grinned. "I told you, Bobby Lee, gangsters don't scare me!"

I groaned. This wasn't going the way I wanted at all.

Just then, Leon showed up, carrying a stack of sandwiches and a glass of milk, which he gave to Terrance. At once Terrance began stuffing a sandwich into his mouth. I wondered how the kid could be so skinny the way he consumed food.

"Why didn't you come back to talk to us after Memphis like we agreed on?" asked Leon, giving me a narrow look. "You thinking of trying to claim the whole reward for yourself, Bobby Lee?"

"Course not!" I said, annoyed that he would think I would betray him. I might not have known him long, and I might have been a thief and a liar, but I wasn't a double-crosser. "I couldn't come talk to you 'cause I've been watched every minute by the folks in that car. But listen, you have to be careful. That Kelly's willing to hurt anyone who interferes, and believe me, I learned it the hard way. He hurt me, he threatened Bujeau—he even threatened Nanette O'Halloran," I said.

Terrance looked up from his sandwich. "He better not hurt Miss Nettie, or I'll take him apart myself," he said fiercely, spraying crumbs with each word.

"I ain't surprised!" Leon said. "Not after what we found back in Memphis!"

He left that hanging. I admit, I left my mouth hanging too.

"What you found?" I asked, dumbfounded.

Terrance giggled. "We went through their luggage in the passenger car, since you couldn't."

"But how?"

"Simple. We told Chelton we'd keep an eye on things so he could step off and have a smoke," Leon said, grinning. "It's against the rules for porters to smoke on duty, so he won't tell on us."

I had to smile at their ingenuity. Apparently, I wasn't the only future criminal on the train. "Well," I said. "What did you find?" I asked.

"Both Bujeau and Kelly are toting heaters in their luggage," Leon said, his eyes glinting with excitement.

My face must have registered confusion.

"That's what gangsters call their guns," Terrance volunteered through a mouth full of half-chewed ham and bread.

"I know what heaters are!" I snapped. "But *both* of them are toting?"

"That's right, but we found plenty more," Leon continued. "Bujeau has markers for horses. He's laid down a whole heap of bets. And he had an accounts book for the Cajun Queen. Maybe he killed Jimmy over a bet."

Hmm. So Bujeau was a gambling man. Was that what

Malcolm had meant when he said Bujeau was better at spending money than making it? I didn't know how it figured in, but I tucked the knowledge away in the back of my brain, in case I needed it later. "What about Kelly?"

"Kelly didn't have much else, just a change of clothes, his toothbrush, aftershave. That kind of thing."

"His aftershave smelled mighty good, though," Terrance said. "See?" He stuck his smooth little cheek up into my face so I could smell him, not that he needed to. He reeked of the stuff. I had thought the smell was coming from one of the trolleys.

I waved my hand in front of my face, trying to clear the air. "If he gets a whiff of you, he'll know you've been in his bags. Seriously, Terrance, he'll hurt you if he finds out."

"He won't find out," Terrance said. "No one pays attention to a couple little Negro boys like us. He won't know a thing."

"Hush up, Terrance. I'm trying to tell Bobby Lee what else we found," Leon said, before turning back to me and continuing. "Nanette has a copy of Jimmy's life insurance policy. It's worth twenty thousand dollars to his wife, or his mother if he wasn't married."

I whistled. Twenty thousand dollars would set a person up for life, sweet as anything. No wonder she was worried that folks might think she was only Jimmy's mistress.

"She had a letter too. From Clovis Dupré, offerin' to take her back into the orchestra, to travel with them around the country. It was written before Jimmy died," Leon said. "Maybe she killed Jimmy so's she could sing with the orchestra again *and* get the money."

"Take that back!" Terrance shouted, so suddenly Leon and I

both jumped. I banged my bruised head on the handle of a trolley and bent over again in pain.

"Take it back! Miss Nettie wouldn't kill anyone! Granddaddy says she has the voice of an angel!"

"Just 'cause she's pretty and sings nice don't mean nothing, Terrance," Leon said.

"She didn't want to go back to the orchestra, Clovis told me that much," I said when the throbbing in my head subsided. "But if she turned him down, I wonder why she's still got the letter."

"Maybe she's planning to go with him if the insurance company doesn't pay her. She has to make a living somehow," Leon said.

I shook my head again. "She wouldn't have to do that. She's half owner of the Cajun Queen, even if she doesn't get the insurance."

Leon shrugged. "All I know is the letter's in her bag."

"Along with some dirty diapers," Terrance said, wrinkling his nose. "They don't smell near so good as Mr. Kelly's aftershave."

Leon rolled his eyes.

"What about the others?" I asked, before Terrance could go into any detail about the diapers.

"They ain't got much," Leon said. "Malcolm Sloan's just got a clean shirt and drawers."

"No gun?" It seemed strange that Bujeau would be carrying a gun, but Malcolm, who was supposed to be his bodyguard, was not. Then again, Malcolm's gun was probably in his jacket pocket.

"Malcolm don't need a gun. He's got all them big muscles,"

Terrance said, making fists and flexing his own spindly frame like a strong man on a circus poster.

"Eat your sandwiches, Terrance. We got to get back on board soon," Leon said.

"And Sergeant Hayworth?"

"He don't have a bag, or if he does he took it with him."

I remembered the sergeant getting off the train in Memphis, his hands in his pockets, giving me that smug nod as he walked by. I understood that nod better now; he had known there'd be a telegram waiting that would tell him the truth about me. "No, the cop didn't take his bag with him. I guess he doesn't have one. So that's everybody," I said.

"Everybody 'cept you," Terrance said, grinning. "You got a prayer book and a rosary. We didn't take you to be such a goody-goody, did we, Leon?"

My face flamed with embarrassment as my hand reached protectively across my small bag. I couldn't believe they had gone through it. That hadn't been part of the bargain. "You had no right—" I said, my words stuttering out on my anger.

Leon grinned too, and held up a small, tarnished silver locket by its chain. "And you had this too. You got a sweetheart, Bobby Lee, or did you steal it?"

"Give me that!" I cried, trying to snatch it.

Leon moved it just out of my reach. "You sure it's yours?"

I lunged again. This time I caught it and pulled it away from him. "It was my mother's," I said, closing my fist tight around it. The powerful longing I'd felt with Nanette and her baby burned through my palm where the locket pressed into it, as if it were a talisman of home. But it wasn't. It was only the last shred of a life that had never found the promised warmth of a real home because of the curse I'd put on it.

Terrance had been grinning at the game, but now his expression turned completely sober. "Is your momma dead?" he asked.

I ignored him, opening my hand to make sure the locket was undamaged. If Leon had broken it, I planned to pound him good, even though he was bigger than me.

"We're sorry, Bobby Lee," Terrance said. "We didn't know. Our momma's dead too."

The locket was unharmed, but I still ignored Leon as he mumbled an apology. The train whistle blew.

"Come on, Terrance," Leon said. "It's time to get back on board. You coming, Bobby Lee? The train pulls out in five minutes."

"I'll be along in a minute," I lied. I should have tried one more time to convince them to stay away from Kelly, but I was too angry at Leon to care what happened to them.

Leon shrugged, and gripping Terrance by a fistful of shirt, he led the way back out of our hiding place. I did not follow. Instead, I scooted all the way back into the dusty corner and leaned against the wall of the phone booth, still burning with anger and embarrassment. If I'd known anyone would go through my things, I wouldn't have brought the prayer book and rosary. I wasn't even sure why I had. They had been on the table beside my bed at the convent, and I had seen them as I was stuffing my few possessions into the bag. On a whim, I had thrown them in. I suppose I had thought having them might make up for taking the money from the poor box. Or maybe I just wanted to have something more to my name than a ragged change of clothes and a broken comb. Either way, it was hardly something an aspiring criminal would carry with him.

I slipped the locket safely into my pants pocket, then I reached into my bag and took out the prayer book. Sister Mary Magdalene had given it to me as we had walked away from my mother's grave. I had never so much as opened it. It wasn't really much of a gift—the Sisters had a ready supply of them on hand to give out to fallen women and other sinners in the Quarter.

I opened the book. The binding gave a soft crack. On the inside of the cover, a slightly crooked stamp read COMPLIMENTS OF THE SISTERS OF CHARITABLE MERCY, and below that their address and phone number. On the opposite page, Sister Mary Magdalene had written *To help you find your way in this difficult time.*

It gave me a little start. Had she known I would run away? No, of course she hadn't. She hadn't meant the words literally.

I angrily tossed the book aside, then leaned my head against the phone booth, turning my ear toward it to protect the tender back of my skull. That's why I heard someone talking excitedly on the other side, in the loud voice necessary over a public line. The sharp Yankee accent caught my attention. I pricked up my ears, but the wood panel was too thick for me to hear clearly what was being said.

I glanced around and saw the empty milk glass Terrance had left behind. I picked it up and pressed the top to the wall of the phone booth and my ear to the base.

"Of course, Mr. O'Banion, don't worry!" Kelly was saying. He paused. "Because I've seen it. It's in her bag." He was silent for a few seconds. "That's right, twenty thousand, which should just about cover it. And she's got witnesses to help her get it." Another pause. "I'm telling you, by Chicago she'll be eating out of my hand. She doesn't trust the others, or won't by the time we get there. Leave it to me. You'll get your money." The next time he stopped to listen, he chuckled. "Well, in that case, we've always got the partner. I don't think either of them will be a tough nut to crack. Don't worry, boss. One way or another, I'll take care of them."

There was another short pause and then the phone clicked down on the receiver. I cowered back as deep into the corner as I could and held my breath as the door of the phone booth opened and Kelly stepped out. I watched through the wheels of the carts as he walked back to the train, cocky as ever.

My guts knotted up with dread as I watched. Mrs. O'Halloran—Nanette—was the nut he intended to crack. He was after her money, and he was making her suspicious of her true friends, if she had any. I didn't know what this told me about Bujeau, but I knew it meant that Kelly was up to no good where Nanette was concerned.

I told myself how glad I was to be getting off the train, leaving all that behind, but I felt only anger boiling up instead of relief. Who did Kelly think he was, stealing Mrs. O'Halloran's insurance money and her chance at a happy home for herself and her baby?

A ticket to Louisville was the answer to all my problems. I could start fresh. But what would happen to Nanette and her innocent little boy if I did? I glanced down at the prayer book. It had fallen open to the Prayer of Saint Jude, patron saint of hopeless causes. A sign from God, plain as day. I didn't know why

God was sending me signs now, when he knew that I hadn't been listening all that well these last thirteen years, but there it was.

I took a deep breath, scooped up the prayer book and my bag, and ran to get back on my train to Chicago.

OHIO RIVER CROSSING, ILLINOIS STATE LINE
8:45 P.M.

Half an hour later I was startled out of deep thoughts about Kelly when the train wheels clattered loudly on the track. I looked out the window to see why the sound had changed. We were on a bridge, crossing a slow, muddy river. The sun had set, but a faint glow still reflected off the water. In the hazy shadows along the banks, the first fireflies were sparking the air.

Soon we had passed over the river and were speeding through flat farmland fading into night. Here the crops had not yet sprouted, and the bare, turned earth gave the land a dull, empty feel. I thought again about what I had heard in Fulton. Kelly had told his boss, "You'll get your money." Why was it his boss's money? Nanette needed that money to raise her baby. Didn't Kelly have a single kind bone in his body? I shifted on the seat, still feeling tender and bruised. I already knew the answer to *that* question.

One thing was clear: money was at the heart of all of this, Jimmy's death as well as everyone's interest in his widow. That twenty-thousand-dollar insurance policy was supposed to protect her, but as far as I could see, it was putting her at risk. But why? Why did Kelly think his boss had a right to that money? And who was his boss, anyway?

I was still looking out the window, mulling over what I knew and what I suspected, when someone stepped up beside my seat. I turned to see Clovis Dupré, accompanied by Leon and Terrance. Leon had put on a shirt under his overalls, and Terrance had tucked in his shirt. Terrance was grinning his oversized grin. My mouth fell open—what were they doing in a whites-only car?

"Beg pardon, Bobby Lee, but Leon and Terrance, who I believe you met earlier in the colored car, they wanted to come back and see you. Folks up yonder are fixin' to retire for the night, and the boys here aren't ready, so I said I'd accompany them to go visiting, if you're not ready to sleep yourself."

"No, sir, I ain't," I said. "But—" I glanced back at the porter, sitting by the compartment door. He was casually ignoring the presence of three colored visitors in the whites-only car. I leaned toward them and whispered, "Are you allowed to be back here?"

Clovis ushered the boys into the seat opposite me, then sat down himself. "Ol' Jim Crow doesn't come to this side of the Ohio River. We're in Illinois now, where colored folks can go anywhere on the train we want. Not that we're really all that welcome, so folks mostly stay put as they are."

Illinois! We had only just entered the state and already things were better! By the time we got to Chicago I figured it would be a whole new world. I still hoped it would be the perfect place for a fresh start. But I knew it would only be perfect if I played my cards right, and I had been dealt a difficult hand.

I glanced past Clovis toward the O'Halloran party. Nanette had been rocking her baby, but she had gone stock still and was staring wide-eyed at my three new companions. I felt a little pang of annoyance toward her. After all, she had shared the stage with Clovis and his band, before Jimmy put up the curtain between them. How could she be offended by their presence in our train car now? I had never understood why upstanding white folks were willing to share their restaurants and stores with a dirty sinner off the streets such as myself, but not a well-dressed, churchgoing colored man. I had asked Sister Mary Magdalene to explain it to me when I was younger, but she had only frowned and said, "We are all brothers and sisters in the eyes of Christ, Robert. Remember that." Which didn't seem to me to be any kind of answer at all.

"You got a lot more room back here than up in our car," Terrance said, glancing around at the nearly empty seats. Since Memphis, we hadn't taken on many new passengers. "Up there folks is gonna have to sleep sittin' straight up. You'll be able to stretch out here. You're gonna sleep real comfortable tonight, Bobby Lee."

I nodded, but I didn't really think so. With what I knew or suspected about the other occupants of the coach, I figured I should stay as wide awake as possible, if I knew what was good for me. I turned to Clovis.

"Mr. Dupré, your orchestra plays at the Cajun Queen, don't you?"

"Sometimes. It's one of the nicest stages in New Orleans, and we always bring in a bigger crowd there than anywhere else."

"Do you always get paid?"

Clovis looked a little offended by the question. "We are professionals, Bobby Lee. We don't ever play for free. Even us jazz cats have to make a living."

"That's not what I meant," I said. "I meant, did Jimmy O'Halloran have the money to pay you as he promised?"

Clovis nodded. "Yessir! Jimmy O'Halloran was an honest businessman, not one of those fellas who figures they could pay less than promised because a black man can't do nothing about it with the law. It's one of the reasons all the bands wanted to play at the Cajun Queen. We were lucky to be a favorite there. Yessir, Jimmy O'Halloran always paid."

"Hmm. I thought he might have been in financial trouble toward the end? That maybe he couldn't pay his bills," I said, a little disappointed that my idea didn't seem to be panning out.

"The place was packed every time we played. They must have been turning a profit. But now that you mention it . . ." Clovis paused, thinking.

"Yes?"

"Well, *Mr. O'Halloran* always paid. But there was a couple of times he left Mr. Bujeau to pay us, and I can't say that he was as reliable as his partner. I know they argued about money. There was one time in particular, when Mr. and Mrs. O'Halloran went off on their honeymoon. He told us he'd be leaving our pay with Mr. Bujeau, but when we went to collect it at the end of the weekend, Mr. Bujeau said he didn't have any money for us. He said Jimmy forgot to leave it, and since it was Sunday, he couldn't go to the bank and get it, so we'd have to wait till Jimmy got back. I couldn't help noticing, though, that Bujeau was sporting a fine new watch chain, all studded with rubies."

"I've seen that chain," I said. "It looks mighty expensive. Do you think he spent your pay on it?"

"Well now, that's not for me to say, is it?" Clovis said mildly.

"We collected our pay when Mr. O'Halloran came back, but he didn't seem all that happy about matters. He went into the office with Bujeau and they stayed in there talking for a long time. Bujeau was the first to leave, and he slammed the door on the way out."

"So it must have been Bujeau's debt and not Jimmy's," I said, not realizing I had spoken the thought out loud until Clovis leaned in closer to me, his brow furrowed.

"What debt is that, son? Nettie's not in trouble, is she?"

"I'm not sure," I admitted. "What about the night Jimmy died?" I asked.

"What about it?"

"Were you playing the Cajun Queen that night?"

Clovis's face clouded as he nodded. "But we weren't nowhere near where Jimmy fell from."

"I didn't mean that," I said quickly. I didn't want to offend Clovis. "I just wondered if Bujeau paid you for that night."

"He couldn't. The police have seized everything while they investigate what happened. The club is still closed. But you said something about a debt?"

I glanced again at Mrs. O'Halloran and her party at the opposite end of the train before I asked my next question. I'd been watching them out of the corner of my eye. Something was up. Nanette had leaned forward and said something to Brian Kelly, whose back was toward us. Now he got to his feet, and for a moment I thought she had sent him to confront us. Instead, he left the car through the rear door without looking our way. Sergeant Hayworth followed a moment later. I turned back to Clovis and asked my next question while I had the chance.

"I just heard something that makes me think Jimmy O'Halloran might have owed someone a lot of money. Mr. Dupré, do you know who Jimmy got his liquor from after Prohibition?"

Clovis frowned and held up a hand to stop me. "That's not the sort of question a person asks, Bobby Lee. Purveyors of fine drink can be mighty touchy about that kind of thing."

I nodded. "I know. But it's important." And Clovis was the only person who might know and who wouldn't hang me off the train by my heels for asking.

Clovis Dupré leaned in closer. I did too, so that our heads nearly touched in the space between the seats. "I won't speak to that, Bobby Lee. I can tell you this, though. The stuff Jimmy was serving wasn't any old bathtub gin. No one else in New Orleans was getting booze that fine."

I nodded, thinking again of the slip of newspaper in my pocket. *More liquor produced in Chicago than before Prohibition.* "Mr. Dupré, have you ever heard of a man named Mr. O'Banion?"

Clovis's brow scrunched down hard over narrowed eyes. "The head of Chicago's North Side Gang? Is he somehow involved in all this?"

"I . . ." I hesitated, not sure if I should repeat what I'd heard.

Before I found the words, Terrance tugged on Clovis's sleeve. "You've got a visitor," he said, grinning.

Clovis and I looked up to see Nanette O'Halloran standing in the aisle, the baby on her shoulder. We came to our feet right away, and Clovis swept his hat off his head.

"Good evening, Miss Nettie," he said with awkward politeness.

"Good evening, Clovis," she replied in a starched, formal tone.

"Please, ma'am, would you care to join us?" I said, gesturing to the seat beside me. She glanced nervously in the direction she had sent Kelly before sitting down. Leon sat down again beside Clovis, but Terrance enthusiastically squirmed his way into the seat between myself and Nanette, so that he was pressed up against her. A scent of jasmine drifted from her rustling skirts as she moved them out of the way for the boy.

"You're mighty pretty, Miss Nettie," he said, smiling up at her. "You used to sing at my granddaddy's Baptist church. He says you has the voice of an angel."

Nanette smiled down at Terrance. "Thank you kindly," she said, "but I go by Nanette now. Nanette O'Halloran. Not Nettie. And I'd appreciate it if you'd keep it to yourself that I ever sang in your granddad's church." She turned to Clovis, and the kind smile she had been giving Terrance disappeared. I realized I had misunderstood her look earlier. It wasn't all colored folk she objected to having in her car on the train. It was Clovis.

"Why are you here?" she said.

"Just came to check up on young Bobby Lee," he said.

Nanette's eyebrows knitted and she gave a tight shake of her head. "You know what I mean. Why are you *here*. On this train. You ought to be in New Orleans. I know you had shows lined up for this weekend."

Clovis began sliding the brim of his hat through his fingers nervously. "The boys and me decided it was time to strike out, make it big. Jazz is hot in Chicago these days, and there ain't enough clubs in New Orleans for all the bands."

Nanette arched an eyebrow, and her lips tightened down. Even through her lacy veil, I could feel the look, and even though it was aimed at Clovis and not me, it still made me squirm. I thought it was just nuns that could pin a fella down that way, but maybe it came natural to all women.

Clovis held up much better than I would have. He flashed her a smile. "There's money in Chicago, Nettie. There's a future for folks like us. Why, if we had a good voice to—"

Nanette stood suddenly, causing Terrance to fall over on the seat.

"It's Nanette now, Clovis. Nettie is gone. And there are no 'folks like *us*.' We aren't the same kind of folks—not anymore. And this business here, it's not your business. You shouldn't have come. You can't help me in Chicago, you can only hurt me! Why can't you see that?"

She was fixing to storm away, but Clovis stood and stepped quickly into the aisle.

"Begging your pardon, Mrs. O'Halloran. I hadn't meant to interfere. If you'll excuse me." He rushed off, back toward the colored car.

Mrs. O'Halloran stayed rooted where she was, breathing hard with emotion.

I rose to my feet too. "You're upset, Mrs. O'Halloran. Please sit down. Can I get you a glass of water? Something to calm your nerves?"

She sat and smiled at me. "Thank you, but no, I will be all right."

"I don't think Mr. Dupré meant to cause offense, ma'am," Leon said. He'd been mighty quiet up until then.

"No. No, of course he didn't," she agreed. "Clovis is a good man. I know that. But I'm not a little girl anymore, who needs taking care of. I'm a widow with a child now."

"But can't you still sing?" Terrance asked. He didn't seem to be following what had happened as well as the rest of us.

Nanette laughed softly and patted her little boy on the back. "Of course I can still sing. Only now I sing lullabies and nursery songs. Folks don't want to hear that in clubs, now do they."

"Will you sing for us?" Terrance asked, once again snuggling up against her.

Leon told Terrance to hush up, but Nanette smiled, situated her baby in the crook of her right arm, and put her left around Terrance. He pulled his skinny legs up onto the seat and squirmed to get more comfortable, kicking me as he did. I moved to the opposite seat where Clovis had been, and Terrance immediately spread out across the space I had occupied, pillowing his head against Nanette's side. She began to sing, her fingers gently stroking Terrance's curly head, to my surprise. I'd never seen a white woman behave so tenderly to a colored child before. It was one more thing to like about her, a woman who put kindness above propriety.

"Hush-a-bye, don't you cry,
Go to sleep, my little baby.
When you wake, you shall have
All the pretty little ponies.

"Blacks and bays, dapples and grays,
Go to sleep, my little baby.

Hush-a-bye, don't you cry,
Go to sleep, my little baby.

"Daddy's boy, Mama's joy,
Go to Slumberland, my baby.
When you wake, you shall have
All the pretty little ponies."

As she sang, I felt Leon relax in the seat next to me. Terrance closed his eyes, a blissful smile on his lips. I turned my gaze out the window and focused on the countryside, now slipping past in darkness. Try as I might, I could not keep Nanette's song out of my heart. It pried its way in, entwining with the grief that I had locked away, tugging out that deep yearning. Her song spoke of family, of safety, of everything coming out all right in the end, and my heart listened and yearned with all its might.

But things weren't like that, not in real life. Sometimes things came out terribly wrong, and a person was left mourning the loss of something he never had to start with. Things like family, and safety, and the promise that everything would come out all right in the end.

Happily ever after hadn't been my fate, or Maman's. It didn't look to me like it was going to be Nanette's either. I thought of sending up a prayer to Saint Jude, but didn't figure he had time for a sinner as unwashed as myself.

"I think they are both asleep," Nanette said quietly when the song ended. I looked at Terrance and Leon. Terrance had slid down so that his head was cradled in Nanette's lap. Leon's head was drooped over the back of the seat, a smile curving his usually tough mouth.

"Good thing my singing doesn't do that to everybody, or I would never have made a living. And I never would have met Jimmy." She looked down into her baby's face with a sad smile.

"Can I ask you something, if it ain't too personal?" I said.

She looked back up at me. "What is it?"

"Clovis says as Jimmy's widow, you're now half owner of the Cajun Queen. Is that right?"

"Yes, that's right," she said.

"So, you'd be okay even if you didn't get the insurance money, wouldn't you? Clovis says the club was always busy. That it had to be turning a profit."

Nanette's eyebrows lifted. "How do you know about the insurance money?"

I shrugged. "I hear things, same as anybody. But you'd be okay, right? With the club?"

She wrinkled her perfect, honeyed brow. "What are you getting at, Bobby Lee?"

I bit my lip. I hated to ask her personal questions. I knew how hard that had been after my mother's death. But I had to know. "I was just wondering why you're going to Chicago at all."

"I told you. My baby boy needs a good home, and I mean to find one for him in Chicago with Jimmy's kin."

"But why not stay with your own kin in New Orleans? It seems like you got something solid in New Orleans, but you don't know what you'll find in Chicago."

She shook her head. "All I've got in New Orleans is a past,

Bobby Lee, and that's not always such a good thing to have. In Chicago, my boy'll have a chance to go far. Make it big. With Jimmy's people, he'll have money, education, opportunity. I don't want to deny him any of that."

I nodded. Of course she would want that for her little boy. I just wasn't sure she could get it with Kelly around. I had to warn her.

I cleared my throat and began again. "Mrs. O'Halloran, was Jimmy in debt? Had he borrowed a great deal of money? Or bought something he couldn't pay for?"

Nanette shook her head. "I don't think so. Alphonse was the big spender. Don't get me wrong—Jimmy treated me in style, and he was generous to a fault. But he had a sensible head on his shoulders too. That's why he was such a good businessman."

"And business was good? Even with Prohibition?" I asked.

"If anything it was better. So many clubs were selling bad liquor, but not the Cajun Queen. Jimmy put quality first in everything, and people knew it."

I thought for a moment. If business was good, I didn't see why the club would owe money to their Chicago connections. Unless . . .

"Mrs. O'Halloran, the newspapers said there was a private party the night Jimmy was killed."

She nodded again. She was chewing her lip now, but she didn't silence me. "That's right," she said.

"I don't think it was a party, was it? I think it must have been some kind of game of chance. For high stakes. Am I right?"

Mrs. O'Halloran glanced toward the seats where her group had been sitting, nervous despite their absence. "I couldn't say,

Bobby Lee. I don't ask that kind of question, and I think maybe you shouldn't either."

Another question I wasn't supposed to ask. But now, all the unanswered answers were starting to add up.

"Look, Bobby Lee," Nanette continued, "it's probably best you not worry yourself over such things. It's not your problem."

"But there *is* a problem?" I asked her.

She smiled, a smile tinged with sadness. "I think it's best if we all get a little rest, don't you? It's getting late, and we've still got twelve hours on to Chicago. It'll go faster if you're sleeping. Good night, Bobby Lee."

With that, she scooted sideways across the seat to get out from under Terrance. The boy was a heavy sleeper and didn't stir, even when she lowered his head to the bench and pulled the last fold of her skirt from beneath his cheek. Then she got to her feet and walked to her own seat.

Leon raised his head off the back of the seat. He was no longer smiling.

"So you think Kelly killed Jimmy because he cheated in a poker game?" he asked.

"I thought you were asleep."

Leon grinned. "I was in disguise. I'm right, ain't I? You think that's what got Jimmy killed."

"Poker, or something else." My mind was racing now. "You said Bujeau had markers for horses in his bag."

"He sure did. A whole lot of them."

"What if Bujeau was betting that night to try to make things right? What if Bujeau gambled away the Cajun Queen's profits while Jimmy was on his last trip out of town? That would explain why he couldn't always pay Clovis and the orchestra. And if he couldn't pay the orchestra, Jimmy sure couldn't pay for the liquor he'd bought from the Chicago rackets. Maybe that private party was Bujeau trying to win it back before the mob took their pound of flesh."

"Say, that is an idea," Leon said, his eyes sparking with interest. "And I know how Terrance and me can find out."

"You do? How?"

"Leave that to us," he said as he stood and stretched. Then he shook Terrance's shoulder to wake him. Terrance muttered and curled up tighter, but Leon kept at him until he opened his eyes and struggled to his feet.

Leon looked back at me and smiled. "See you later, Bobby Lee," he said, and set off for the colored car, Terrance staggering along behind him. They were gone from view before it occurred to me that Leon might be planning something dangerous.

NORTH CAIRO, ILLINOIS
9:23 P.M.

Night was settling in by the time we stopped in North Cairo, Illinois. Sergeant Hayworth walked casually up the aisle toward the door. As he passed me, he gave a sharp jerk of his head to indicate that I was to follow him. I didn't want to, but I didn't want to get into Hayworth's bad graces either. Not when I had passed up my single best chance to get away from him. I would have to cooperate with him enough to keep him from turning me in. So, once he was off the train, I stood and stretched, gingerly unknotting my bruised muscles. Mrs. O'Halloran had gone off to join Mr. Bujeau and Malcolm after I'd talked to her, and Kelly hadn't returned, so none of them could see me talking to the sergeant.

I stepped off the train and glanced around, momentarily confused. Passengers were milling around to stretch or smoke, the black folks all mixed in with the whites. I'd never seen anything like it. Even as I stood disoriented by the steps, a colored family walked past me and boarded the very car I'd been riding in, normal as anything.

Hayworth was waiting for me a few steps up the platform, out of view of the car's windows, glaring impatiently at me as I gawked. I hurried to him.

"Well, kid? What have you got for me? You've passed the time with both Bujeau and LeBlanc. What did you find out?"

"Mrs. O'Halloran doesn't know anything, and she's not up to anything. She's going to Chicago to give her boy a good home with her husband's relatives," I said with conviction.

Hayworth huffed and rolled his eyes. "I didn't take you for the type to be suckered in by a pretty face so easily."

I gritted my teeth to hold back my anger. I hadn't intended to tell him much of anything, but the instinct to protect the mother and baby overpowered both my criminal intentions and my good sense. "Bujeau is in debt, I think. He's been betting on horses and buying things he can't afford. I think he's gotten himself and the club into money trouble."

Hayworth shook his head. "I *know* all that, kid. I got that from sources back in New Orleans."

"You know that? Then what do you need me for?" I was compromising everything to give him information he already knew? He was even more of snake than I had thought.

"I told you, I need you to find out how they plan to scam folks in Chicago once they get there."

"Who says they're scamming anyone?" I said. "Jimmy got his bootleg through his connections in Chicago. It's Kelly you should be after, not Mrs. O'Halloran. I think he's the one that killed Jimmy, because those connections hadn't been paid off for all the liquor Jimmy was buying from them. And he's the one that's planning to do something awful once he gets to Chicago."

"He's outside my jurisdiction, kid. My job is to crack down on the crooks and swindlers like Bujeau and LeBlanc in New Orleans."

"But they're not crooks—or at least she's not. And she may be in trouble in Chicago. Kelly's planning to steal all her money, or worse. I heard him on the phone with his boss."

"Oh yeah? And who is this boss of his?" Hayworth asked with a smirk. He'd forced me into ratting out a gangster with the threat of returning me to New Orleans, or worse, and now he wasn't even going to believe what I told him. That made me madder than a treed possum. I squared my shoulders and looked him in the eye. "Mr. O'Banion is his name."

Hayworth's eyes grew wide and the smirk melted off his lips. For a moment I thought it was because I had convinced him of the danger. Then he leaned in close to me, grabbing a fistful of my collar and lowering his ugly face to mine.

"Look, kid, I'm not gonna say it again. Kelly and his lot ain't my problem. Cops have ended up dead poking their noses in there, and I have no intention of joining their number. So you'll forget whatever you heard and you will *not* put me in the middle of it."

"I thought you wanted to catch whoever killed Jimmy O'Halloran."

"I'm expected to bring someone in to stand trial for Jimmy's murder. Bujeau and LeBlanc have as good a motive as anyone. He had debts. Maybe they were having an affair. Maybe they needed to get Jimmy out of the way. Is that what you heard, kid?"

I stared at him, my mouth falling open. Could he really mean to pin the murder on Alphonse and Nanette, just because he was scared of Kelly and the North Side Gang?

"But they're innocent!" I protested.

"Ain't nobody in this world who's innocent," Hayworth replied. "There's just those who ain't been caught yet."

"But it's murder! They'll hang!"

"That's not your concern, kid."

The whistle blew, making my head ache, and the conductor shouted his all-aboard. Hayworth let go of my collar and stepped back. "Just find out what I need, kid. Find out that they're lovers. Get her to admit Jimmy wouldn't marry her. Something useful. Once I've got that, I'll have enough to take them in."

"But—" It was no use talking; he had already turned and was walking away.

"I won't help you do that!" I shouted after him.

He glanced back at me and flashed me a dangerous smile. "It's either them or you, Bobby Lee."

I stood a moment longer, too outraged to follow, but the conductor shouted and waved a hand at me, and there was nothing to do but board the train. When I entered the train car, Hayworth and I were the only ones on it—at least the only ones involved with Jimmy O'Halloran and the Cajun Queen. The others must have gone to the dining car or one of the lounges. The black family that had boarded was still busy with getting their luggage and their children settled in. As I started to sit, I saw Leon signaling me from up ahead, so I went to see what he had discovered.

"You were right," he said when I stepped through onto the platform between the two cars. "Look at this!"

He held out a slender, leather-bound book and I opened it. The pages were made of ledger paper, and had mostly been filled in with accounts, kept in a solid, confident hand. He flipped pages until he came to the last one with entries.

"What is this?" I asked, though I had a sinking feeling I knew.

"Remember I told you Bujeau had the accounts for the Cajun Queen?"

"You *stole* his accounts book?" I said. Talk about sticking a finger between the tree and the bark!

"Naw, I just borrowed it. I just mixed myself in with that colored family yonder and no one noticed what I was doing. But look." He held it closer to my face for my inspection.

Columns of numbers showed the club's profits and also its debts. Beside each debt was a notation, showing when it had been paid. But halfway down the page, the notations of payment ended, even though the bills continued to mount and the income kept rolling in.

"See?" Leon said, pointing to where the payments ended, about a month before Jimmy's death. "He was in debt, just like you said. He wasn't paying for all these big charges listed as 'Misc.' I figure that's another word for bootleg, don't you? Strange, 'cause the club seemed to still be making money."

I let my eyes scan along the profits, thinking about what Clovis had said, and about the ruby watch chain and the many rings on Bujeau's fingers. I thought too of Malcolm's words. Bujeau was better at spending money than making it.

"Those markers you saw in Bujeau's bags. How much were they for?"

Leon shrugged. "Too much to count. I'd say hundreds of dollars, maybe more."

I nodded slowly. My hunch had been right. Jimmy O'Halloran had been connected to one of Chicago's most powerful gangs. That's probably how he'd had the money to start the club and certainly how he had kept it supplied. But Bujeau had gambled away all the profits and then some, and Jimmy hadn't had the money to pay for the bootleg he'd already bought. So Kelly, who worked for that powerful gang, had been sent down to get payback of one kind or another. I guessed that Bujeau and Jimmy had done what anyone would have done in such a dangerous situation: stalled. Promised a big return on a poker game that night.

I could practically picture the scene, all of them in that room, crowded around the table, the room stuffed to the gills with high rollers. When it was clear Bujeau wasn't going to come through with the money, Kelly had started the tussle that sent Jimmy off the balcony. A balcony Kelly had prepared, knowing that the game was the Cajun Queen's last chance to pay up.

Now, if Nanette didn't get the insurance money and turn it over to Kelly's boss to pay off the bootleg, he might be planning the same end for her and Alphonse Bujeau. And the cop traveling with us, the one person who could do something about it, would do nothing. In fact, he wanted to send Bujeau and Nanette up the river for a crime they didn't commit. Just went to show, there were crooks on both sides of the law.

"It was Kelly then?" Leon said. He'd put it together too. "Do you think he'll hurt Miss Nettie?"

"I don't know," I admitted.

"Well, you've got to help her!" Leon said.

I knew he was right. I also knew I was in the stew. I couldn't just let poor Nanette and her baby end up in the clutches of either a killer or a dirty cop, but how could I hope to help her and not ruin my chances of criminal prosperity in Chicago? All I could think to do was to let her other companions know what both the cop and the gangster were up to. Surely Bujeau and Malcolm would protect her if they knew Kelly's plan, and if I was careful, Kelly would never know I had tipped them off. They could be the heroes without me being branded a snitch.

"Should we go to the police?" Leon suggested.

I shook my head and told him what Hayworth had said on the platform. Leon made a face.

"Dirty copper," he said.

"But we can tell her friends what we know," I said. "Bujeau, Malcolm, Dupré. If we warn them that Kelly is the killer, they will protect her. Bujeau owes her, seeing as how it was his debt that got Jimmy killed."

Leon nodded. "You talk to Bujeau and Malcolm, and I'll talk to Clovis. Surely someone will help her."

I agreed and parted company with Leon, a new possibility buzzing in my head. All I had to do was tell Bujeau what I had learned, and he would do the rest. He would assign Malcolm to protect her, which Malcolm would do, seeing as how he was fond of Mrs. O'Halloran from way back. Then, I could slip away at the next stop with a clear conscience. I paced the length of the aisle twice, as if stretching my legs, then I paused at the end, where a porter sat on duty.

"What's the next stop?" I asked him.

"Anna, Illinois, sir, but there ain't nothin' much there. Round midnight we'll be comin' in to Carbondale."

"And there's more there than in Anna?"

"Yes, sir, though I reckon it'll all be closed, 'cept the main station. We'll be making connection there with the line to and from St. Louis, so there's always some activity."

The line to St. Louis. That was the perfect escape. "Midnight, you said? What time is it now?"

The porter drew his watch from his pocket and flipped it open. "A quarter to ten, sir."

I thanked him and returned to my seat. I had plenty of time. I would wait, and maybe Hayworth or Kelly would drift off to sleep. Then I could get Bujeau aside and warn him. Then I'd step off the train in Carbondale and never look back. And with all I'd learned since setting out that morning, I figured I could set up in the crime business in St. Louis just as well as Chicago.

Smiling to myself, I leaned my head gingerly into the corner by the window, cushioning it on my bag, and I closed my eyes. Like Leon, I figured pretending to sleep would be my best disguise until I could make my move.

MAY 28, 1923
CARBONDALE, ILLINOIS
12:02 A.M.

The lurch of the train woke me from sleep. At first I thought we must be coming into the station at Anna, but then I realized the train was not slowing to a stop, but starting up again. I hadn't meant to sleep at all, but had apparently missed the stop at Anna entirely. Still, it didn't matter, as I had most of an hour till Carbondale. I went to the lavatory. When I stepped out again, the porter smiled at me.

"Were you able to take care of your business in Carbondale, sir?"

I stared at him. "My business?"

"You were asking about Carbondale earlier. I hope you found what you needed there?"

"But we haven't gotten there yet, have we?"

"Why, yes sir. That was Carbondale back yonder where we just pulled out."

"Was it?" I felt my heart sinking down into my toes. "When is the next big stop?"

"Big stop, sir?"

"Where there are connecting lines and more than just a train station."

"I can't say as how we have another stop like that until Chicago. Besides, it's past midnight. Things'll be pretty shut up tight most places till we get on to Champaign, round about four o'clock. There's usually coffee and pastry ladies on the platform there. After that, it's just a couple hours on to Chicago. Was there something specific you were needing, sir?"

"I don't need anything," I said. I turned back toward my seat and surveyed the compartment. Sergeant Hayworth was asleep. Nanette had removed her hat and veil and cushioned her head against her bag to sleep. I could not see the baby, so I assumed he was asleep in his basket, and Kelly, with his back to me, was reclining in the seat opposite her. Bujeau and Malcolm, however, were elsewhere.

"Do you know where those two gentlemen have gone?" I asked the porter, pointing to their seats.

"Gentlemen who can't sleep often go to the smoking lounge," he said.

I thanked him and went looking for them. I passed through the sleeping train, the aisles dark and the bunks curtained off in the Pullman sleeper cars. I found both Bujeau and Malcolm in the smoking lounge. Bujeau was at a table with three other men, playing poker. Malcolm stood watch behind him. A large pile of money was in the middle of the table, and three more piles sat in front of the three other men, but not in front of Bujeau. Bujeau had taken off his jacket and hung it over the back of his chair, and large rings of sweat showed at his armpits. All the signs were there—he was getting fleeced. The big roll of cash he'd flashed me was most likely gone—just like the profits of the Cajun Queen. And that made me as mad as a cat.

"What do you think you're doing?" I shouted.

The men at the table all flinched, then glared at Bujeau once they figured out I was with him. Bujeau jerked his head toward the door and growled, "Take care of him," and just like that, Malcolm had me by the shoulder and was pushing me back the way I'd come, into the observation car beyond.

"But it ain't right," I protested. I wanted to say more to Bujeau, but that's all I could manage before Malcolm had me out of earshot. He pushed me down into a seat, towering over me in case I tried to bolt.

"Why do you let him gamble?" I shouted at Malcolm. "Bujeau's gambling got Jimmy killed!"

He said nothing, his face expressionless as stone, his body telling me how close I was to getting flattened.

After a few minutes of silence, Bujeau came through from the next car, his face red and glossed with sweat.

"*Nom de Dieu*, you rotten brat! What do you mean, barging in on a big game like that! I could have lost a bundle because of you!"

"You already lost a bundle, didn't you? And what you didn't lose, you spent on expensive jewelry you don't need!"

"What are you talking about!"

"That's what got Jimmy killed! When he couldn't pay the North Side Gang for the booze he'd bought."

Bujeau's eyes went wide and he jerked back from me in surprise. "The North Side Gang?" He shook his head and a small, humorless smile tugged at the corner of his lips. "I knew he had good connections, but I had no idea they were that good. Jimmy played his cards close to the chest." He shook his head again and muttered, "You were a fool, Jimmy. A brilliant fool!"

"You must have known," I said.

"Like I've told you before, kid, there are some questions you don't ask. Jimmy said to leave it to him, and I wasn't sticking my finger under the bark of any tree that involved bootleg from Chicago."

"But surely you suspected Brian Kelly when he showed up demanding payment," I persisted.

A guilty expression flickered across Bujeau's face, but then he remembered he'd been reading me the riot act. "Look, kid, whoever Jimmy knew, he'd known them long before he met me. It was cutting deals with the likes of the North Side Gang that got him killed, and that ain't none of your business."

I rose to my feet, but Malcolm pushed me back down into the chair. "That's what you were doing that night, wasn't it?" I demanded. "You'd gambled away the profits, so Jimmy couldn't pay. So when Kelly came down in person to collect, you tried to make money the only way you knew how. But you lost and Jimmy took the fall!"

"I was trying to win back the money to bail Jimmy out!" Bujeau said. "Jimmy was a good partner, and a good man. I didn't want him to get hurt."

"That's why you've got to help Mrs. O'Halloran, Mr. Bujeau. If she doesn't get the insurance money and can't pay Mr. Kelly, he might hurt her. Kill her even. You can't let that happen when the debt was yours and not Jimmy's. It's bad enough you got him killed."

"Saying things like that could get *you* killed, boy. You're to say Jimmy O'Halloran's death was an accident, and I don't expect to hear anything else about it out of your mouth. I thought I'd been clear on that point."

"But Nanette is innocent!" I said.

"Don't kid yourself. Everyone on this train has an angle, Bobby Lee; everyone is looking to profit one way or another. Yourself included."

"You can't let a widow and child pay for your mistake! It's bad enough what happened to Jimmy but—"

"*Maudit enfant!* Stay out of it! Keep your mouth shut and collect your money, you hear? Nan's a swell kid and it's tough luck for all of us, but they'll kill me if they don't get that money. Nan will get by fine, everybody loves her. Do you know what it's like to get people to trust an old Cajun off the bayou? Do you see folks stumblin' over themselves to help me out? It's like you said, kid, *Chaque chien hale sa couene.*" There it was again: every dog has to carry his own hide. And Bujeau was a dog if there ever was one.

"But—"

"Now Malcolm will see you back to your seat. And if you interfere again, I'll have him see to it that you won't be *able* to interfere by the time we get to Chicago, *n'est-ce pas*?"

Malcolm grabbed a fistful of the back of my shirt and hoisted me to my feet. With little pushes every few steps, he started me back from car to car. When we got to the empty dining car, I spoke.

"What about you, Malcolm? You said Miss Nettie was blameless. Are you going to let her get killed now that you know the truth?"

"What truth is that?" Malcolm said. He still had a firm grip on my shirt, but he had stopped walking, which gave me some hope that he would listen.

"I heard Kelly on the phone in Memphis. He killed Jimmy, and I think he would kill again if he had to, to get the money."

Malcolm's eyebrows rose. "You heard him say he killed Jimmy?"

"Not exactly," I admitted. "But it's the only explanation—"

Malcolm let go of my shirt. "What exactly did you hear, son?"

I repeated the phone conversation as best I could remember it.

"So you didn't actually hear him say he meant to harm Mrs. O'Halloran?"

"Well, not in those exact words, but that's what he meant."

Malcolm gave me another little push and we started walking again. "You'd best follow Mr. Bujeau's advice and just stay out of it, Bobby Lee. You're only making things more dangerous by interfering. You're making people nervous, and when people get nervous, accidents happen."

"But someone's got to help Nanette!" I said. "I thought you were her friend."

"I am. But Mr. Bujeau is my boss, and this is business. Now get back to where you belong," he said, giving me one last little push but not following. "Go on." He was doing me the favor of letting me return the rest of the way on my own. It was the only favor he would be doing me.

I straightened my shirt and my shoulders and, with one last reproachful look that I hoped would at least make him feel guilty, I turned and walked away.

CENTRALIA, ILLINOIS
1:15 A.M.

I crept through my own car, where everyone was sleeping, and on to the lounge car beyond, in search of Leon and Terrance. Terrance was wrapped in an old quilt, his head bobbing in and out of sleep, but Leon was talking with Clovis Dupré, both of then wearing tense, tight expressions.

"Did you talk to Bujeau?" Leon asked the second I slid into the seat opposite them.

"He's no help," I said. "He already knows Kelly is after the insurance money, but he doesn't care. He figures it's the best way to get the Chicago mob off his back."

"But it was his debt that got Jimmy killed, not Miss Nettie's," Leon protested. "He should have to pay it back on his own."

"He's scared of the North Side Gang. Of O'Banion. They all are," I said.

Clovis shook his head. "I never much trusted that shifty Cajun, but I didn't think he was such a coward that he'd let a woman and baby pay for his mistake. 'Specially not Nettie."

"What about you, Mr. Dupré? Can you help her?" I asked.

"I would if I could," he said. "I just don't see as how she'll let me. She told me to steer clear, remember? You heard her yourself."

"But she doesn't know the trouble she's in," I said, the desperation and frustration rising and pushing my voice up with it. "She doesn't know, and no one's willing to help!"

"Now calm down, son. It ain't that I'm not willing. There just ain't that much I can do until she'll let me. Maybe if you tell her what you've heard, let her know what kind of trouble she's in, you can make her change her mind. Maybe she can help herself."

"Help herself how?" I asked. I was willing to do most anything that might save her from Kelly and get this yearning out of my confused heart.

"She could go to the police. She could give me and my boys a chance to help her. But it has to come from her. I can't step in if she won't let me."

I nodded. "Thank you, Mr. Dupré. I'll talk to her first chance I get," I promised.

"And tell her me and the boys are at her service. She just has to say the word," he said.

I returned to my seat, hopeful that I had at last found a solution and eager for my chance to act on it. Back in my car of the train, everyone was still asleep. I was considering waking Mrs. O'Halloran to talk to her when a squall rose from the baby's basket. Everyone in the car stirred at the sound, but the men all burrowed their heads deeper into the coats or bags they were using as pillows and kept their eyes shut.

Nanette, yawning, took Jimmy Jr. into her arms and shushed him. He quieted to a demanding fuss. Nanette picked up her bag and moved to an empty seat farther from the sleepers. She changed the baby's diaper, then lifted him to nurse him. This, I realized, might be my best chance to talk to her, but I was too embarrassed to approach while she had the baby to her breast. I turned my face to the window to give her privacy, but my eyes kept wandering back in her direction. I glanced back at her companions too. Was Kelly really asleep? His back was toward me and I couldn't be sure. If I told Mrs. O'Halloran what I knew and Mr. Kelly was awake, or if he woke up and caught me, I'd be in the soup for sure. I couldn't risk it, but maybe I could catch her eye and get her to meet me in another compartment. Unfortunately, all her attention was on her child.

The train slowed as it approached another station. Out the window I could read the sign: CENTRALIA, ILLINOIS. The final jolt of the stop brought a wail of protest from Jimmy Jr. Nanette put the child up over her shoulder and stood, but he protested louder. She walked the length of the aisle to the sleepy porter behind me.

"How long are we stopped here?" she asked.

"Only 'bout fifteen minutes, ma'am," he said.

She nodded. "Maybe in the fresh air he'll settle down," she said, patting the baby's back.

"Yes ma'am, but don't go far," the porter said, opening the door for her and offering a hand down the steps.

I glanced around the compartment. No one else had stirred. As quietly as I could, I slipped out of my seat and off the train. The platform was deserted but for myself and Nanette, who was pacing back and forth, singing softly to soothe the baby. She saw me and gave me a little smile, but continued singing. I waited a few minutes while Jimmy Jr. settled into silence. Then I approached her.

"Mrs. O'Halloran. I'm sorry to bother you, but there's something you have to know."

Her gentle face crinkled with concern. "What is it, Bobby Lee? Are you in trouble?"

"No, ma'am, but I'm afraid you might be."

Her face relaxed. "Because you've heard that Jimmy was murdered?

"Sergeant Hayworth wants to pin the murder on you. He thinks you and Mr. Bujeau planned the murder together."

"He can't pin something on me that I didn't do. And I've got Alphonse and Malcolm looking out for me too."

I shook my head. "I'm afraid not, Mrs. O'Halloran. That's why I have to warn you." Quickly, I told her what I had pieced together: that Jimmy had been killed by the Chicago North Side Gang because he couldn't pay Bujeau's debt, that Bujeau was tricking her into giving him the club, knowing that she would lose the insurance money to Kelly, and finally that Kelly would hurt, or even kill, whoever stood in his way of collecting the cash. She listened with a serious expression as it all spewed out of me.

Then she shook her head. "You shouldn't worry so much, Bobby Lee. These things aren't your concern. My old friends won't betray me or let me walk into a nest of vipers like you've described."

"But Clovis Dupré—"

"You've told Clovis Dupré all this?" she said, her expression suddenly annoyed.

"He wants to help you, Mrs. O'Halloran, if you will let him."

"I don't want his help." Her face had gone hard, even as a sheen of tears rose in her eyes.

"But—"

"Bobby Lee, I appreciate what you are trying to do, but again, you don't understand as much as you think. If you want to help me, you'll not interfere. My best chance is to join Jimmy's family in Chicago."

"I don't know if Jimmy's family can protect you if the Chicago mob is after you. And from what Sergeant Hayworth said, I don't think the police will either. I heard Mr. Kelly on the phone in Memphis. He was talking to his boss. He said—"

I broke off suddenly at the sound of footsteps behind me. I turned just as Mr. Kelly himself appeared out of the darkness.

"Ah, Nanette," he said, smiling right past me at her. "I see little Jimmy Jr. is sleeping again at last. I hope Bobby Lee isn't disturbing him. Let sleeping babes lie, that's what I say."

Nanette smiled at him. "No, Bobby Lee was just keeping me company and making sure I was safe out here alone in the middle of the night."

"Well, wasn't that nice of him." He turned his smile toward me. A chill ran along my spine as I read the truth in his eyes. He'd heard everything I had said, and from the weighty lump in his jacket pocket, I guessed he'd come prepared to do something about me once and for all.

"But it is very late, and the baby's asleep now," he said, turning back to Mrs. O'Halloran. "Shall we get back on the train? You should get some rest too. Things will be busy in Chicago, with Jimmy's funeral and all. And you will want to be at your best to meet his family."

She nodded. "I suppose you're right. We should all get what sleep we can."

Kelly offered his elbow to Nanette and escorted her to the train. With gentlemanly politeness he assisted her as she mounted the steps. Once she was on board, he turned to face me, standing between me and the train.

My mind was racing, and I said the first thing to come into it. The first thing I thought might save my skin. "Mr. Kelly, I won't tell anyone! I swear! In fact, I can help you get what you're after."

"You've done enough, kid. In fact, you've interfered for the last time," he said. His hand dropped into his bulging jacket pocket.

That uprooted my feet, right quick. I turned and ran up the platform, past the baggage car and the engine. I didn't look back to see if he followed. I kept to the shadows, expecting to hear or feel the gunshot at any moment. Beyond the engine, the platform ended and the rails ran on into the darkness. I could see buildings, but it was too dark to know whether or not they could provide me a hiding place. I jumped down from the end of the platform, stumbling a little as I landed on the uneven ground. Regaining my footing, I leapt across the track in front of the engine, then looped back around the other side of the train, putting it between me and Kelly. I hoped he wouldn't leave the platform for fear of missing the train himself.

I had thought the entire train station was deserted, so I was surprised to charge into a crowd on the other side of the train. In fact, I was so surprised that I couldn't stop in time, and I crashed into a tall porter.

"Ho, there! Careful!" he said, staggering backward and

grabbing my shoulder to keep us both from falling. "What's your hurry?"

I tried to break free of the man's grasp, but his grip was strong. I looked around, frantic. There were nearly a dozen porters, drinking coffee and smoking cigarettes. The old white-haired porter from the colored car was there. He stepped forward, his wrinkled face crinkling with concern.

"This here's the boy my grandsons have taken a shine to," he said.

"Let me go! I gotta get away!" I said, jerking my shoulder again, trying to get free. All I could think about was running as far and as fast as I could.

"What kind of trouble you in, son?" the old porter asked.

"There's a man—a gangster—trying to kill me," I said, still struggling.

The old porter and the one who held me looked at each other, and for a moment I thought they didn't believe me. Then the old man pulled open the door of the baggage car.

"In there. Quick," he said, and the man gripping my shoulder steered me toward the door.

I didn't need to be told twice. I made a leap in and over some trunks and ducked down. Just in time, too. A moment later I heard Kelly's sharp Yankee voice addressing the porters.

"You see a kid run through here?" he asked. "'Bout so tall, ragged clothes. Shifty eyes."

"No, sir," said a porter, his voice bland and polite.

"You sure? He ran in front of the train—looked like he circled this way. I'm just trying to get him home to his momma, you understand," Kelly said.

"Ain't seen nobody," the porter said.

There was a long pause. I held my breath. The train whistle blew.

"Train's pullin' out soon, sir. Best be getting on board," the porter said, his voice still steady and polite, revealing nothing.

I heard Kelly grumble, but he seemed to be walking away.

I waited, not sure whether they would make me get out of the baggage car or not, but no one said anything to or about me. I stayed where I was, flat on the floorboards behind some heavy trunks. A few long minutes passed before I heard some scuffling. Then the door closed and I was in complete darkness.

I began to get up, but then I realized I wasn't alone. I could hear someone breathing. The train shuddered and jerked once, then began rolling forward. There would be no escaping the train, the baggage car, or whoever was in there with me now.

SOMEWHERE IN ILLINOIS
TIME UNKNOWN

I lay perfectly still. It seemed the safest thing to do. If Kelly was my unseen companion in the baggage car, my best chance was to remain hidden. The darkness in the car was complete, and that was to my advantage. I just had to remain silent, keep still, and hope he didn't stumble across me.

At least, that had seemed like the best plan. Until I heard the scrape of a match on a nearby trunk, and a moment later a lantern flared to life, casting long, wavering shadows around me where I lay facedown on the floor. Still, I didn't move. It seemed unlikely lying still would save me now, but I didn't know what else to do.

Someone stepped around the trunks beside me, and a booted foot prodded my leg.

"You dead?" Terrance asked.

I shot to my feet, propelled by surprise and relief.

"Terrance!"

Leon was standing behind him, holding the lantern high and grinning. "Granddaddy told us you was in here. Thought you might like some company," he said.

All I could do in response was nod. I was afraid if I opened my mouth, my heart might jump right up and out of it.

"Come on," Leon said. "There's usually room toward the back. We've got three hours on to Champaign, we might as well get comfortable."

They led the way over and around trunks and crates, suitcases and canvas bags of mail. Fewer trunks crowded the back corner, just as Leon had said, and we shifted them around to create a cozy little space where we could all stretch out together to sleep. We didn't lie down right away, though. I wasn't sure I'd ever be able to sleep again after the fright they'd given me. I was too keyed up and jumpy to even think of sleep.

I guess Terrance and Leon felt the same way, because they sat down on crates and boxes and looked at me, as if waiting for a bedtime story. I didn't say anything. I knew they wanted the details of what had happened, but I didn't want to think about it, let alone repeat it for their entertainment. They weren't letting me off the hook that easily, though.

"Who was chasing you, Bobby Lee? Was he really trying to kill you?" Terrance asked.

"It was Kelly, and yeah. He was trying to kill me."

Leon looked skeptical. "Did he try to shoot you? I didn't hear no shots."

"He had the gun in his pocket, and he reached for it. I didn't stick around to see what he did after that."

"Well, you're safe here, Bobby Lee," Terrance said.

I nodded. "I'm mighty glad I ran into y'all's granddad. Otherwise, I'd be stuck back there in Centralia, or worse." I didn't really want to think about the worse.

"And you'd never get to Chicago to see your Yankee aunt," Terrance said.

"Don't you get it, Terrance?" Leon said. "There's no aunt in Chicago. He's right off the streets, just like we thought."

"Is that true?" Terrance asked.

I nodded. "It's true. I was heading to Chicago in hopes of joining up with the criminal element, but I don't see that there's much chance of that happening now."

"But . . ." Terrance said, his little face scrunching up with concern. "But you're no criminal, Bobby Lee."

I shrugged. "How do you know what I am?"

"'Cause we're friends," Terrance said, looking hurt.

"So? Seems to me you're criminals too."

"We are not!" Leon said, bristling. "Just you take that back, Bobby Lee."

"You're not supposed to be on the train," I pointed out.

"That don't make us criminals!"

"And you snooped in the baggage."

"That was your idea!"

I shrugged. "I guess nobody's really honest in this world. 'Cept maybe little babies like Jimmy Jr."

"Well, we're not hurting nobody. Not taking advantage either. I don't see why you'd want to be like them. Why you'd want to take money from widows and babies."

Now it was my turn to bristle. "I don't! I want to help Nanette O'Halloran. I just don't see how I can."

Leon raised his eyebrows like he didn't believe me. "Why, so *you* can take her money instead? You said before you don't even know her."

"He wouldn't take her money, would you, Bobby Lee?" Terrance said. "You fell in love with her right off."

"I did not!" I said, though I could feel my face turning redder than a crawfish in a gumbo.

"Sure you did. Everybody does," Terrance said. "Clovis says she's the sweetheart of the jazz scene."

"Not everyone," I said, thinking again about the sharp expression that never quite left Kelly's eyes.

"I bet that's how it was for Jimmy O'Halloran too," Terrance continued. "One look and he was mad in love, don't you think, Leon?"

"I don't know. I reckon you should ask him, not me," Leon said. Terrance and I both looked at him, confused. With a mischievous grin, he nodded at the box under Terrance's skinny backside. "You're sittin' on him."

Terrance leapt up like there were hot coals in his underpants. In an instant he had crossed the open floorboards and wedged himself into the little space available between Leon and me. Sure enough, the long low box on the other side of the sleeping space we'd made for ourselves was the pine coffin I'd seen them load in New Orleans.

"I've been sittin' on a dead man?" Terrance whispered, his eyes huge as saucers.

"You don't have to whisper. You won't wake him up," Leon said.

"Are you sure?" Terrance said, still in a whisper. "I've heard the dead wake up after midnight sometimes. 'Specially them that's been wronged."

"Well, why don't we open the box and see," Leon said, getting to his feet. "Who knows what he can tell us. We'll need a crowbar to get the lid off. Must be something around here that'll work."

Terrance pressed himself hard against me, trying to bury his head under my arm or behind my back. "I've never seen a dead person before," he whimpered.

"That ain't true, Terrance. You saw Momma laid out."

"But she didn't sit up and talk," Terrance said, still trying to burrow.

"I bet you've never seen a dead person either, have you, Bobby Lee," Leon taunted.

"I saw my Maman too. And some babies at the Sisters of Charitable Mercy."

"You seen dead babies?" Terrance said, peeking out from under my arm.

I nodded. "Sometimes women who don't want their babies leave them on the doorstep at night for the Sisters to take care of. But sometimes before the nuns can find them—" I shrugged. "Babies need a lot of care, you know?"

Terrance pulled his head out from under my arm. "Why wouldn't a lady want her baby? Our momma always said her babies was her whole world."

"My mother would have been better off if she'd gotten rid of me," I said. "She'd have had a better home, better food. She wouldn't have been so poor all the time."

"Pops always said we was eating 'em out of house and home, that's why we was poor. But Momma said everything else about us made 'em rich. I bet your momma felt the same way," Terrance said.

I shook my head, but memories flooded back, of all the times Maman had left good positions so she could be with me. I had thought I'd been nothing but a stone around her neck all those times, but maybe she had been *happier* with me. Maybe she'd felt the same yearning that I'd been feeling and been pulled away from those jobs by it, just like how I'd let it ruin my chances for a new life in Chicago because I fell for Mrs. O'Halloran and her baby.

"It's ladies with no husbands who have to get rid of their babies, Terrance," Leon said.

"Have to? Why?" Terrance asked.

Leon was poking through a toolbox in the corner. "They just have to, that's all. You'll understand when you're older."

Terrance frowned. "Will Miss Nettie have to get rid of her baby? She ain't got a husband."

"But she had one," I said. "It's different. She's a widow. It's ladies who were never married who have to give up their babies."

"But she weren't married," Terrance said.

"Of course she was. To Jimmy O'Halloran," I said.

"They weren't," Leon said. "They couldn't've been."

"Why ever not?"

"Granddaddy says old Jim Crow won't let colored folks marry white folks," Terrance said.

I stared at Terrance, confused. "Jimmy O'Halloran was black?" I said.

Terrance giggled.

Leon straightened from the toolbox with a big grin on his face and a crowbar in his hand. "He wasn't black, he was Irish. But I bet he's kinda blue or green by now. Let's find out."

Terrance let out an earsplitting screech and burrowed his head back under my arm.

"Leave it alone, Leon," I said.

"You chicken, Bobby Lee?"

"No. But you're gonna give Terrance nightmares something fierce."

Leon sat down on the coffin, looking contrite. "I was just foolin', Terrance. The dead don't rise after midnight. He's just laid out in there in a fine suit, all ready to go into the ground. It's the famous Jimmy O'Halloran himself! Don't you want to see?"

Under my arm, Terrance's head shook vigorously back and forth and a little whimper escaped.

Leon seemed to be weighing the crowbar in his hands, deciding what to do. I decided changing the subject was the best course of action. Besides, I was still confused.

"What did you mean about white folks and colored folks?" I said again.

When I looked at Leon, he was smirking again. "She's fooled you good, ain't she?"

"What are you talking about?"

"Nanette LeBlanc is colored."

"No she's not," I protested.

"Sure she is," Leon said. "Why else would she be singin' in our granddaddy's Baptist church and performing all over town with the Clovis Dupré Orchestra? She's colored folk, same as Terrance and me. That's why Jimmy O'Halloran couldn't have married her."

I shook my head. "But I've seen her," I insisted, but even as I said it, I was seeing her rich, black hair and beautiful full lips in a different light.

"She's an octoroon," Terrance said. "One-eighth Negro."

Leon nodded. "Granddaddy can remember back before Jim Crow, when Creoles like her lived on the other side of town and mixed with white folks, easy as pie. But now white folks don't figure that's right. They figure even one drop of colored blood makes a person black. And there's colored folks in her family back a ways."

"So you're saying even though her skin is white, she ain't?" I said. "That makes no sense."

"It don't have to make sense, it's the law," Leon replied. "She's only been white since Jimmy O'Halloran asked her to be."

"But—didn't folks know?" I asked.

"All the colored folks in the Eighth Ward know. Ain't no keeping secrets there. But white folks don't take the trouble to know us folks in colored wards. There's some advantages to being invisible sometimes," Leon said. "So when she started stepping out with Jimmy, I reckon there was some whispering here and there, but white folks didn't know for sure that she was colored, and black folks weren't telling."

I thought about that and about why she'd said she didn't want to stay in New Orleans. She had a past, she'd said. I thought she'd meant life on the stage, but now I saw she couldn't stay. Too many folks knew the truth—folks who had been willing to look the other way for Jimmy's sake, or for their own convenience. But they wouldn't look away for long now that she was a woman on her own. As soon as the white folks of the city realized she was black, she'd lose everything. If she wasn't legally married to Jimmy, she had no claim to the Cajun Queen.

"She sure fooled me," I said. "I couldn't see any reason why she and Jimmy wouldn't have been married."

"I guess she has to fool Jimmy's people in Chicago the same way. If she can fool them, she'll make herself white for good," Leon said.

"Do you think Sergeant Hayworth knows?" I asked.

"Could be. If he's been investigating Jimmy's past, I'm sure he's been digging around hers," Leon said. "Folks from our part of town don't necessarily file all their doin's with the courthouse, babies and marriages and such, so he probably can't prove her family's past with paperwork. But it wouldn't be too hard to find out through word of mouth. Plenty of folks saw her onstage with Clovis Dupré before Jimmy started segregating her at the Cajun Queen."

I nodded, thinking. Hayworth was looking to pin Jimmy's murder on someone. Nanette and Bujeau were both in his sights, but the more I thought about it, the more Nanette seemed to be the easier target. Digging around Nanette's past, Hayworth probably had enough evidence to make a good case that Nanette and Jimmy had never married—but not being married wasn't a crime. So he was waiting for her to commit one. Claiming to have been married to Jimmy so as to receive insurance money, like she planned to do in Chicago—*that* was a crime. And as soon as she made the claim, Hayworth would have her.

Of course, if she *didn't* claim the money and usc it to pay off Kelly, *Kelly* would have her.

The only way out for Nanette LeBlanc was to find a way to prove she and Jimmy were legally married. I recalled Hayworth's orders to me: *I need you to find out how they plan to scam folks in Chicago once they get there.* This must have been what he meant—how Nanette planned to convince Jimmy's folks she'd married their son. But proving that looked to be impossible. I doubted the testimony of Bujeau and Malcolm would carry enough weight. And even if they all testified that they had witnessed such a wedding, Hayworth could then arrest her for trying to pass as white and marrying a white man, which was illegal. And what would Jimmy's family do if they learned she was one-eighth black? I didn't know if that mattered in Chicago. After all, in Illinois, blacks were allowed to mingle with whites on the train. Did that mean Yankees didn't care about that kind of thing? Did it mean that Nanette really could have been married to Jimmy if they had met in Chicago instead of New Orleans?

I supposed it didn't matter. Once Hayworth heard her make the claim to marrying Jimmy in New Orleans, either she was lying to defraud the insurance company, or she was admitting to an illegal marriage. My blood boiled at the thought. She had loved Jimmy. They had a baby together. She *deserved* the life-insurance money. That was what it was for, taking care of his family after he died. Making sure they would be able to fulfill that powerful longing without it destroying them.

It wasn't right that a few drops of Negro blood should deny people love and comfort. Nanette had mingled with rich white society and with poor black folks, and everywhere she went *everyone* loved her. Now they would all despise her when she was dragged back to New Orleans unmasked. People would judge her by some stupid law about a few drops of blood rather than by the warmth and beauty they'd experienced in her company. And once they all despised her for her lie, how hard would it be for Hayworth to get her convicted of murdering Jimmy for the money so she could continue the deception?

She would be hanged for her crime, and poor Jimmy Jr. would end up an orphan, probably at the Sisters of Charitable Mercy. No wonder my prayer book had fallen open to the Prayer of Saint Jude. This was about as hopeless a case as I could imagine, and the only way out that I could see would be divine intervention—something a sinner like me hardly dared ask for.

I did know one person who had God on her side, but if I called upon her aid, I'd end up right back under her thumb. I wanted to help Nanette, but was it worth my freedom? My bright, criminal future?

I pulled myself out of my thoughts and glanced again at my companions. Despite his fear, Terrance had rolled himself in a blanket and gone to sleep.

"Are we closed in here now, all the way to Chicago?" I asked Leon.

"They'll open up the baggage car in Champaign. Plenty of folks get on and off there, as well as a heap of mail. That ain't until about four thirty or five, though, so we best bed down now and get a few hours of sleep."

We settled Terrance more comfortably, pillowed on Leon's shirt. Then Leon and I stretched out beside him and Leon blew out the lantern.

The baggage car was utterly black inside. I lay awake, staring blindly into the darkness, unable to close my eyes.

"I ain't a criminal, Bobby Lee," Leon whispered after a while. "Since our momma died, there's been nobody to take care of Terrance. And since Granddaddy's rheumatism got so bad in his back, he can't do his job proper. I might be breaking the law by being on this train without a ticket and helping

Granddaddy out, but that don't make me a criminal. I got a family that needs me."

"I know, Leon," I whispered back. "I'd do the same thing in your shoes."

"I know," Leon said. "'Cause you're no criminal neither. That's why you want to help Miss LeBlanc."

I didn't answer. I just let the words slip away into the darkness. He was right, on both counts. Now all I could do was send up a prayer to Saint Jude, and hope Nanette LeBlanc was praying too.

CHAMPAIGN, ILLINOIS
4:05 A.M.

I woke to the grating rumble of the heavy baggage door being pulled open. The thin, gray light of predawn filtered in, then lanterns filled the car with light and a cold gust of wind, colder than New Orleans in January. We had arrived in Champaign, Illinois, the last stop on the line before Chicago. My last chance to try to find help for Nanette. I had come up with a plan, or at least an idea, though it would mean risking my own freedom. The problem was, to pull it off I needed my prayer book. Which was in my bag that I'd left on the train. I hadn't figured out exactly how to retrieve it without being caught by Kelly.

Just then, the big porter who had helped me into the baggage car appeared from around a pile of luggage, carrying a tray of food in his hands and my bag over his shoulder. He set the tray of food on the coffin.

"Rise and shine, boys. Your granddaddy sent you some breakfast. We've got an hour here, then two and a half on to Chicago, but he's gonna need your help toting the heavy things once we get there, Leon. So y'all need to eat up before then."

He handed me my bag. "Since it appeared you had left the train, the porter in your car collected this as lost luggage."

"Thank you, sir," I said, taking it from him. At once I felt the hard edge of the prayer book through the worn fabric. Sometimes, the way things worked out, I had to wonder if Sister Mary Magdalene worked for God, or the other way around. I pulled the prayer book from my bag and slipped it into my pocket. Terrance, once he had rubbed the sleep from his eyes, told Leon that he needed to pee, so the three of us made our way into the station with that excuse.

A surprising number of people were milling around inside, white folks and black folks and all with the quick impatience I associated with Yankees. Apparently, quite a few folks went into the city to work for the day. They were eager to board, briefcases and toolboxes in hand and the morning news under one arm. I accompanied Terrance and Leon to the bathroom. Then I told them I would see them back on the train and went my own way. A row of three wood-and-glass phone booths occupied the far wall. I glanced around cautiously. No one was watching me, so I cut across the room and closed myself into one of the booths. I opened the prayer book to the address and phone number stamped on the inside of the front cover. It was only a little after four a.m., but I knew the Sisters would be up, starting their day. I took a deep breath, lifted the receiver from the hook, and dropped my last coins into the slot. It did not take long for the operator to connect me, but the phone rang for a long time before anyone picked it up. After the fourth and the tenth rings, I almost chickened out. Finally, after the twelfth ring, someone answered.

"Sister Mary Magdalene, please," I said.

"She is in the kitchens, very busy. May I help you?"

"This is Robert E. Lee Claremont. She will want to talk to me."

"Robert! Oh, thank the Lord! Robert! Stay on the line!"

The Sister set the phone down with a clunk, and I could hear her shouting excitedly to find Sister Mary Magdalene. Apparently, my disappearance had caused quite a stir. I couldn't help a little smile at the thought. My smile vanished quickly, however, when Sister Mary Magdalene picked up the phone.

"Robert! Where on earth are you? Are you in trouble?" her tone was as stern as ever, and my back and shoulders straightened automatically, even though she was hundreds of miles away.

"I'm not in trouble," I said. "Not exactly. But I need your help."

"Where are you?" she asked again.

"Champaign, Illinois, on my way to Chicago. And I'm not in trouble, but a friend is, and I need a favor." The words tumbled out as I explained to her about Nanette and her baby, about the debt Alphonse Bujeau had run up that had gotten Jimmy killed, and the killer, Brian Kelly, who still intended to get repayment out of Nanette in Chicago. Finally, I explained to her about Sergeant Hayworth and his plan to arrest Nanette and pin Jimmy's murder on her.

To her credit, Sister Mary Magdalene listened to my whole explanation without interrupting once. But when I paused at the end to catch my breath before asking the favor, she jumped in.

"Robert, have you taken up with criminals?"

"No, ma'am. They're on my car in the train is all," I said, relieved she hadn't asked if I had *intended* to take up with criminals. Lying to Sister Mary Magdalene wasn't easy.

"Have nothing more to do with them! Stay right where you

are, Robert, and I'm going to find a priest or nun there in Champaign who can take you in."

"No, listen!" I said, trying to keep my voice steady. "I'm going on to Chicago. But I need a favor. Nanette O'Halloran needs proof that she and Jimmy were married. And Jimmy was Irish, so he must have been Catholic, right? I need you to verify that they were married in the church."

"I have no way of knowing that, Robert. Anyway, it's not our concern. Now, stay—"

"It *is* my concern!" I was almost shouting. I took a deep breath. I had to be respectful with the Sister. "If she can get the insurance money and be accepted by Jimmy's family, she will be all right. She won't have to be out on the streets, struggling for a living like Maman. Her baby won't grow up being a noose around her neck, like I was to Maman."

"Robert—"

"Please, Sister. I know I don't deserve a favor, but do it for her. Do it for that innocent baby. You know what their life will be like if you don't."

"So you're asking me to lie, Robert? So that a woman who has borne the fruits of her life of sin can defraud those around her?"

"She's a good person," I insisted. "She would have married Jimmy—they wanted to marry—but that stupid law said they couldn't. And you've always told me we're all brothers and sisters in God's eyes. So it's the law that's the sin, not Nanette's love for Jimmy, right? Didn't Jesus say to give unto God what is God's and to Caesar what is Caesar's? And Jesus said to love, right? So they should have been allowed to marry by God's law, shouldn't they? They *loved* each other."

"Do not twist Our Savior's words for your convenience, Robert. This is a matter of law. Even if I did say they had been married in the Church, this policeman could still arrest her as you said, and declare the marriage invalid."

"But what if they were married north of the Ohio River, where there ain't no Jim Crow laws? Would it be legal then?"

"Aren't," she corrected. "And they weren't."

"But would it have been legal? She's only one-eighth black—she doesn't even look black."

The Sister let out a heavy sigh, something she eventually did in every conversation we had. "I suppose it might have been, I don't know. But Robert, you know it's a lie. And lying is a sin. We've talked about this before."

"It would be a greater sin to condemn people to a life like Maman's. Like mine! Aren't we supposed to forgive? To love our neighbors? Aren't we supposed to be good Samaritans?" I was getting desperate and drawing up every Bible lesson I could think of that might apply. Unfortunately, I hadn't always listened to her lessons, so I was running out of arguments.

"Robert, I appreciate what you are trying to do. But this is not your concern, nor mine. It is a matter for the police to decide. Now listen to me. I need you to stay exactly where you are. I am going to find someone to meet you there at the station to keep you safe, and I am going to wire them money to get you a ticket back home. Stay right where you are so they can find you, do you understand?"

"No! I'm going on to Chicago. *Someone* has to help that baby and his mother. Maybe it's a sin, but I know it's the right thing to do."

"You can't help them, Robert."

"But I can try! And I won't have a clear conscience unless I do!" With that I hung up the phone, even though I could hear her starting to speak. I waited a moment in the phone booth, expecting a bolt of lightning to strike me dead. When it didn't, I turned to open the phone-booth door. There, on the other side of the glass, stood Nanette LeBlanc.

CHAMPAIGN, ILLINOIS
4:42 A.M.

I opened the door and stepped out.

"Bobby Lee! Thank goodness! When you didn't get back on the train in Centralia, I was so worried about you. Where have you been?" said Mrs. O'Halloran.

"With Leon and Terrance," I said, proud of myself for avoiding another lie. "Listen, Mrs. O—Miss LeBlanc. I tried to tell you before, you are walking into a trap in Chicago. If you get the insurance money, Kelly plans to take it. If you don't, he might hurt you. And either way, Sergeant Hayworth plans to pin Jimmy's murder on you. He knows you couldn't of married because he knows . . ." I didn't know how to say it. It seemed utterly foolish, when her skin was as fair as mine, to call her colored. "He knows the truth about you."

"I know," she said, placing a gentle hand on my arm to calm me.

"You *know*?"

She nodded. "It's not a secret that can be kept in New Orleans. And I'm sorry you've been drawn into the thick of it. From the moment we left New Orleans, everyone's tried to use you. It was wrong of all of us, and ever since you got hurt, I've been trying to think of a way to get you out of it."

"But you are going to get hurt too. How can I help you?" I said.

"I knew the risks before I ever got on the train," she said. "I knew that Sergeant Hayworth had most likely figured out the truth about my past, and if he had, he wouldn't let me get away with the insurance scam."

"But it's not a scam, is it?" I protested. "You did love Jimmy enough to be his wife, didn't you?"

"More than enough."

"You'd have married him if you could have, right?"

She nodded. "If only we'd met in the North, where I could be legally considered white, we would have done it properly."

"And your baby is his son. And isn't that who the life insurance is supposed to protect? If Sergeant Hayworth pins Jimmy's murder on you, you will hang!"

She nodded, looking pale. "I know. That is why I had to take my chances on this trip. It's not so much what happens to me that I'm worried about. It's Jimmy Jr. Even if the O'Hallorans won't accept me, even if I'm arrested and taken back to New Orleans, I'm hoping to convince them to raise my little boy. If they will take him in, he can grow up with all the privileges of a white man. That's the best gift I can give him."

"But he needs his mother!"

She shook her head. "With me in New Orleans, he will have nothing. He'll be somewhere between white and colored, same as me, not fitting in anywhere, and with no opportunity to advance himself. I chose to pass as white because I loved Jimmy, and I had to be with him. But now that I've lived in the freedom of that world of privilege and wealth, I can't deny my son that life. I can't take him back to New Orleans to work the docks.

A white Yankee family can give him opportunities I never dreamed of."

"But—"

A train conductor walked through the depot, ringing a hand bell announcing time to board. I looked at Nanette, a knot of dread in my stomach. There was no way out for her in Chicago.

"Get off the train now, Mrs. O'Halloran," I said. "Take your baby and your things and slip away from all of them now. They won't know where you've gone. Go somewhere else and start a new life completely."

She shook her head again. "Kelly's friends would find me. The only skill I have is my voice, and they have connections in every club for hundreds of miles. And I could never give my boy a good life by doing laundry or waiting tables. He's what matters now, Bobby Lee. But you should stay out of sight the rest of the way to Chicago. If Kelly doesn't know where you are, he'll forget about you. You're just a kid, not enough of a threat to matter. And thank you for trying to help. You are a kind soul. Now get back to wherever you've been keeping yourself." She gave me a kiss on the cheek. "I hope your aunt in Chicago treats you real fine."

So that was that. She turned and walked back to the train. I had achieved nothing. Sister Mary Magdalene was not going to help me, and my hopes for my future in Chicago were all dashed. I had gotten myself on the wrong side of a gangster and given away my escape for nothing. All that waited in Chicago now was disaster. But Sister Mary Magdalene, like her boss, worked in mysterious ways, which probably meant she already had someone headed to the Champaign train station to retrieve me. I'd be caught for sure if I stayed, so there was nothing to do but go on.

CHICAGO, ILLINOIS, END OF THE LINE
7:47 A.M.

The remaining two and a half hours stretched out endlessly. Terrance and Leon had eaten most of the food before I returned to the car, but I didn't care. I was too worried to eat, and too angry, too. I was angry at Nanette for walking into the trap in Chicago, and angry at Sister Mary Magdalene for refusing to help. I was angry at Hayworth and Bujeau and Kelly. Come to think of it, I was angry at the whole world.

After filling up on the food, Terrance and Leon went back to sleep. So I sat alone in the dark, stewing. Sister Mary Magdalene had always said to take comfort in prayer at times like this, but how could I take comfort in a God that would punish love—Nanette's love for Jimmy and for her baby, Maman's love for me. If there was a God, I was angriest at him most of all.

We rolled on in darkness, ever closer to the final stop. When the train slowed, I knew we were moving through the city. I could hear the whistle blowing its warning as we crossed street after street. I gripped my bag and waited. At last, we eased to a stop. Chicago, Central Station. The end of the line.

The train gave its final gasp and settled. What was I going to do? There would likely be a nun or a policeman looking for me—I wasn't sure which the Sister would have sent. Nanette would be meeting Jimmy O'Halloran's family, and Kelly—who would he be meeting? I didn't want to think about that, and I certainly didn't want to run into them. I wanted to just blend into the crowd and disappear. But if I did, what would become of Nanette?

The baggage-car door was pulled open and a flood of bright sunlight momentarily blinded me. Beyond the door I could hear the noise of a big crowd. It wouldn't be hard to lose myself among them, and I knew that was the best thing to do. Despite all my efforts, I could not help Nanette, and to try again would only put me in reach of Brian Kelly. So, as soon as my eyes were adjusted to the light and I could see clearly, I made my escape. I didn't even say goodbye to Leon and Terrance. I'd never been much good at goodbyes, and I didn't figure I'd be any better at it now that I had friends. So I just pushed the bag of candy I'd bought in Memphis into Terrance's hands and jumped down to the platform. Leon called after me as I walked away, but I didn't look back. I wanted to make my escape into the city quick and painless—and alone.

The platform was packed with people hugging, shouting, and waving. I worked my way through them, trying to avoid contact with anyone. Several archways led from the platform into the enormous station, and I examined them carefully. Sure enough, a nun was standing just under the central arch, watching the crowd. Fortunately, there were smaller side entrances, and I couldn't see a nun or a cop in the one closest to me. I made directly for that one, falling into step just behind one matronly looking woman as if I belonged with her. It probably would have worked, if I hadn't glanced back and spotted Nanette O'Halloran. She had been met by a somberly dressed group—an older, bent woman in old-fashioned mourning clothes, a younger woman, also in black, and a group of six men, all strikingly alike in build and features.

Without thinking, I turned to watch. Nanette was standing before the older woman, her head bowed respectfully, while the old woman inspected the baby, pulling the blanket back from his tiny face with a gnarled finger.

Jimmy's family, for I assumed that's who they were, didn't seem to be taking kindly to the idea of a wife and baby they had never heard of before. They looked severe and sober as they took in Nanette and her child. The old lady did not coo or stroke the baby's cheek. I could see no sign of affection at all.

I glanced at the crowd behind Nanette. Bujeau, Malcolm, and Kelly were all standing a respectful few steps away from the family. Sergeant Hayworth was hovering as well, a hungry look on his face, like a stray dog outside a butcher shop.

It wasn't going well for Nanette—someone had to help her. I didn't know what I could do, but I knew I had to try. I took a step toward them, but got no further. A hand suddenly clamped onto my shoulder.

"You must be Robert Claremont," said a stern female voice. I turned and looked up into the face of a nun. Beside her stood a policeman. I looked back to where I had seen the nun at the main entrance, wondering how she had snuck up on me so fast. The other nun was still there, watching the crowd. Of course, Sister Mary Magdalene had been clever enough to send an army of nuns to catch me. And the police too.

There was no point denying who I was. I had given myself away, watching Nanette's group with interest, and besides, nuns could smell guilt a mile away. My best defense now was to be meek and cooperative, in hopes of sneaking quietly away later.

"Yes, Sister," I said. "But please, before I come with you, there's something I have to do."

"Then those people over there must be your friends from the train? Mrs. O'Halloran, I believe?" she continued, as if I hadn't spoken.

"Yes, ma'am," I said. I was surprised Sister Mary Magdalene had shared so much information with her.

"Well, come along, then. The sooner we get this over with, the sooner we will be able to get you back safe and sound to the Good Shepherd House. Really, Robert, you have done a very dangerous thing, running away. Maybe you didn't know, but Chicago is full of criminals—it's not a safe place for a boy alone."

She continued to grip my shoulder and lecture as she steered me back into the thinning crowd on the platform, toward the O'Halloran party. A glance over my shoulder told me the policeman was accompanying us also.

Kelly was the first to see us approaching. He glanced from me to the police officer, then back to me, murder in his eyes. I fought down the urge to break from the nun's grip and bolt for the exit.

The nun, perhaps unaware of all the looks of curiosity, annoyance, and hostility directed our way, glided through the crowd and directly to the O'Halloran family, pushing me along before her.

"You must be Mrs. James O'Halloran," she said, as we stepped up to Nanette and the old lady.

"Yes, that's me," Nanette said with a curious glance at me.

"My dear, my sincerest condolences at this time of loss. I will pray for the soul of your departed husband, and that you might find solace in Our Lord and Savior Jesus Christ at this time," said the nun.

"Thank you," Nanette said.

I held my breath. Had she dragged me back under the nose of Kelly and Sergeant Hayworth just to offer her condolences?

That was the moment that Sergeant Hayworth chose to make his move. He stepped forward, a look of triumph in his face, and addressed himself to Jimmy's mother.

"Mrs. O'Halloran, let me offer my condolences as well, on the death of your son. I am Sergeant Hayworth, of the Louisiana State Police. I'm afraid, Mrs. O'Halloran, this woman was not Jimmy's wife—were you, Miss LeBlanc? She is preying on your grief to try to force herself and her illegitimate child on you!"

Nanette flinched at the word *illegitimate* and pulled Jimmy Jr. protectively close.

"Ah, Sergeant Hayworth," said the nun. "Just the man I wanted to talk to. I am Sister Bridget of the Sisters of the Good Shepherd. I received a call this morning that you might be arriving, and that there was a matter of some confusion regarding the marriage of Miss LeBlanc and Mr. O'Halloran."

"There is no record of such a marriage ever taking place," Sergeant Hayworth said. His expression had changed to one of wariness as he regarded the Sister.

"Well, there wouldn't be in New Orleans. But I received a call this morning from St. Joseph's Church in Cairo, Illinois, confirming they were married there in secret"—the Sister took a quick glance at the baby—"a little over a year ago."

My mouth fell open, and for a moment I thought my eyes might pop right out of my head. I had just heard a nun tell a lie! Fortunately, no one looked my way before I could close my mouth and blink my eyes back into shape. They were all staring at the Sister.

"Cairo, Illinois?" Hayworth said, looking furious. "An interesting choice. Why on earth would they have married there?"

Nanette smiled, glancing at me. I was glad we'd talked in Champaign, so she knew my thinking. "Jimmy was a Yankee at heart, Sergeant, so you'll understand he wanted to marry *north* of the Mason-Dixon Line."

"And is there a record of this marriage?" Hayworth growled. I admit I had to admire his courage, growling at a nun, but maybe it was just the desperate sound of a trapped animal.

"I am assured by Father Dominic that it was recorded in the church records. They will send documentation to us as soon as they can, sir. It should only take a few days."

"And has it been filed with the state of Illinois?"

"No," Nanette said. She looked at the elder Mrs. O'Halloran. "Jimmy's family was important to him. We married in Cairo, to be joined in the eyes of God, but Jimmy wanted to wait until we could come to Chicago and do everything properly in front of his family."

The older Mrs. O'Halloran's stern face softened slightly. "If Jimmy was married in the Catholic Church, he was married," she proclaimed with an air of authority.

Hayworth was glaring at Nanette, absolutely seething. "Married or not, Mrs. O'Halloran, there's something else about Nanette LeBlanc you should know. She's—"

The Chicago cop who had arrived with Sister Bridget interrupted. "Pardon me, Sergeant Hayworth, but I've been sent from the Lower East Side Precinct with an urgent message from your captain. It seems they have a new suspect in Jimmy O'Halloran's killing in New Orleans, and you are needed back there right away. You are to take the next train back. I believe there is one departing in about twenty minutes."

He held out a telegram. Sergeant Hayworth unfolded it and read it, looking like a kettle getting up a full head of steam as he read. He gave one last nasty glance at Nanette and Bujeau and stalked angrily away.

Jimmy's mother was looking at Nanette suspiciously. "What is it he was going to tell me? What else should I know about you?"

Nanette blushed prettily behind her veil. "I am—or was—a Baptist, Mrs. O'Halloran. But I converted before we married."

My mouth fell open again. If Leon had been there he'd have called her a smooth operator for sure. I had a momentary doubt about her innocence, but I looked again at the baby and clamped my mouth down tight.

Sister Bridget cut in. "I've asked the priest in Cairo to send a certificate, Mrs. O'Halloran, so you can file it with your insurance company. I expect I'll have it in a few days, if you would care to drop by the convent and pick it up. Now if you will excuse me, I must be getting this one back." She tightened her iron grip a little harder on my shoulder.

"Thank you, Sister," Nanette said. "And thank you, Bobby Lee, for all your kindness. I do hope you will come to the funeral if you can. It would mean a great deal to me to have you there."

I tried to look appropriately solemn, despite the relief almost knocking me over. "Yes, ma'am. Thank you. Goodbye," I stammered.

Sister Bridget immediately steered me away, before I had time to judge the reaction of any of the others. They had to realize I'd had something to do with what had just happened, even though I hadn't said a word through the whole thing. I hoped they were all satisfied by this turn of events, and realized the part I'd played in the whole con. Then maybe Kelly'd decide not to kill me. Maybe he'd even consider recommending me to his boss. At the moment, however, there was nothing for me to do but go wherever Sister Bridget's iron fist was taking me.

She hauled me through the station, a cavernous, echoing building of white marble, and out the doors onto a busy street. Cars zoomed by, more traffic than I'd ever seen in New Orleans, where half the vehicles were still carriages and buggies. What was it about Northerners that made them always in such a hurry?

A whole battalion of nuns met us outside. They hailed several cabs and I was soon zooming off at breakneck speed through the traffic toward the House of the Good Shepherd Convent and Orphanage. It was the first time I'd ever ridden in a car, but I couldn't rightly enjoy it, squished in as I was among a whole pack of Sisters.

"Thank you, ma'am," I said to Sister Bridget once I recovered my wits. It was too late for a first impression, but it wouldn't hurt to get off on the right foot all the same.

"For what?" she asked. "I do only the Lord's work. No more, no less."

"Did Sister Mary Magdalene tell you about Nanette's predicament?"

"She told me about you, young man, and that you can be a slippery one. I have been advised to keep a close eye on you until someone arrives to escort you back to New Orleans. And to keep a close eye on the poor box too. I expect you will want to spend your time here meditating on your sins. Stealing from the poor box is stealing from widows and orphans. Is that the kind of person you want to be?"

I didn't answer—not out of obstinacy, but because the question brought me up short. What kind of person *did* I want to be? I'd been telling myself I wanted to be a criminal to get rich. But the truth was, I'd figured it was my future. Not because it's what I'd wanted so much as because it's what I thought I already was.

But now, this nun had asked me—asked *me*—what I wanted to be. And to be honest, I'd never thought about it this way before.

As a choice. As *my* choice.

Suddenly, for the first time in my life, my options were wide open before me. And I wasn't entirely sure which one I'd choose.

MAY 29, 1923
NORTH SIDE NEIGHBORHOOD, CHICAGO, ILLINOIS
10:25 A.M.

The funeral was a somber affair, as I suppose all funerals are. It took place in a handsome Catholic church in the Irish neighborhood on the north side of the city. The simple pine box in which Jimmy's body had traveled was replaced by an elaborate casket of polished wood set with brass fittings. Lavish flower arrangements were piled on the coffin and displayed all around the altar. I went in the company of Sister Bridget. It hadn't been hard to convince her to take me. Nuns will get a fellow into church any way they can. Afterward, however, she was eager to return to the House of the Good Shepherd. It was Nanette who saved me, by inviting us to the wake.

"I must be getting him back," the nun said from over my shoulder.

"I can see to it that he gets safely back to the convent, Sister," Nanette said. "It would mean the world to me to have you there, Bobby Lee. I know so few people here." Her eyes were troubled and my heart ached.

Sister Bridget considered a moment. "I can wait for you here, if you promise to come straight back from the wake. And no more than an hour," she said, giving me a stern look.

My innocent looks and my good behavior since meeting her at the train station were paying off. I promised, not too worried about whether or not to keep the promise. I didn't know what opportunities could come to a fellow at a funeral, but if she lost me because she trusted me, I figured that was her own fault, not mine.

The wake was at the O'Halloran family house, a few blocks from the church. I walked there at the back of the crowd, and soon found myself in the company of Clovis Dupré and his orchestra.

"I ain't never been to an Irish wake. How about you?" he asked.

I shook my head. I'd never been to a wake at all. After Maman was buried, the Sisters had gone back to their usual chores with no further fuss.

"Well, they say there's plenty of music, and Nettie has asked the boys and me to bring our instruments, so I guess that means we're going," he said, holding up a trumpet case to show me.

"Well, Clovis," said a man with a trombone case, stepping up beside us, "this here's your last chance to win her back. If you don't try now, you'll never see her again. Is that the way you want it?"

"They've got them a rich white Yankee family now. You know I can't offer them anything to compete with that," Clovis said.

"It's a shame. A voice like hers could have been famous, what with phonographs getting so popular, and the jazz craze in New York," said the trombone player.

"Life on the road ain't what she wants, Del. And I don't blame her," Clovis said. Then he let out a deep sigh. "I've seen her safely here. Now I'm gonna get out of her life and let her live it as she sees fit."

I looked up into his face. His eyes sagged under the weight of his regret.

"Mr. Dupré, do you love her?" I said.

He smiled a little. "Everybody loves Nanette LeBlanc, son. You should know that by now. Even you, and you only met her two days ago."

"But, I mean, you loved her even more than that, didn't you."

Clovis didn't answer, just focused his eyes far away up ahead.

"He loves her with his whole heart and soul," Del the trombone player said. "He asked her to marry him, and she was considerin' it when she met Jimmy. It broke Clovis's heart, I can tell you."

"Now, Del, we don't need to go dredging all that back up," Clovis said.

"The boys and me, we think Clovis ought to fight to get her back. We're tourin' the country, and we'd be mighty pleased to have the lady singing with us again. The band ain't been the same without her, and ol' Clovis here, he can only sing the blues these days."

"So it wasn't a coincidence that you were on the train with them after all," I said. "I knew it couldn't be."

Clovis shook his head. "None of us rightly knew what she'd encounter here in Chicago. If Jimmy's family didn't accept her and she didn't get her insurance payment, I didn't want her to be all alone. But she's got everything she wanted. A nice white family to raise her nice white baby boy."

We walked the rest of the way in silence—Clovis with his trumpet, and me with the disturbing feeling that despite all my schemes, I'd managed to get it all wrong.

Inside the O'Halloran mansion, I quickly became separated from Clovis and Del as I was ushered into the front parlor. More large sprays of flowers crowded the room, their sweet odor making the warm air oppressive. The chairs and sofas were all occupied by women and a few children, looking stiff and uncomfortable in their starched Sunday best. In the corner, a gaggle of cooing ladies hovered over little Jimmy Jr. in his lace-covered bassinet. Old Mrs. O'Halloran was being congratulated by friends on how beautiful and healthy the baby was, as if he were her child and not her grandchild. They were also offering their condolences to the old lady.

Nanette sat in a stiff-backed chair a few feet away, but no one congratulated or consoled her. It was as if she were an invisible island in the crowded parlor. She wasn't invisible to me. I went directly to her and sat down beside her. She gave me a grateful smile. "I'm glad you came. I didn't have a chance to thank you properly back at the train station."

I shrugged, feeling embarrassed. "It was nothing."

A mischievous twinkle lit her eye, and for a moment I almost saw the girl she had been before the world had smothered her with grief.

"Getting nuns to lie for you? Hardly seems like nothing. In fact, you may be the best con artist of any of us, pulling that off."

I shrugged again, embarrassed and flattered that she'd noticed. "Clovis Dupré really gave me the idea. He told me how the laws in the South about colored folks don't apply up here in the North, so I figured there was at least a chance that they could marry white folks up here."

"They can't," she said, and a flash of anger passed over her face. "But up here, an octoroon is considered white. In Louisiana, one drop of Negro blood makes a person a Negro."

We paused in our conversation as a small group of women moved past us to get closer to the baby, who had now been lifted out of the bassinet and was being displayed proudly by one of Jimmy's sisters.

"Do you like your new family here, Mrs. O'Halloran?" I asked.

She gave me a thin, brittle smile. "They took to Jimmy Jr. right away. They are already discussing nannies and schools, and a job in the family business. He will be very well taken care of here, I think."

"What about you?" I asked.

"Don't worry about me. I will have a roof over my head."

I frowned, looking at the stiff way the women turned their backs on us where we sat in the corner. "They don't seem like a very nice family. Do you think they know about your secret?"

"Mrs. O'Halloran had been planning for Jimmy to marry higher up on the social scale—a banker's daughter, perhaps. But I have his son, so they will allow me to stay for his sake."

I looked again at Jimmy's mother and sisters on the sofa. Above them, a framed cross-stitched picture hung on the wall. The words HOME IS WHERE THE HEART IS filled the center of frame, all wreathed with fussy little doves and flowers in silk thread. I thought of how unfussy and warm things had felt when I was with Terrance and Leon on the train. When it felt like they had welcomed me into their family. I turned back to Nanette and gripped her hand.

"Clovis Dupré would still take care of you, you know. He loves you. You could marry him and you'd have a family in the orchestra."

She shook her head. "Clovis can't offer my baby the same kinds of opportunities he'll have with the O'Hallorans."

"But he can offer love and family. The kind of family that hugs and laughs and feels warm and safe, no matter how many fleas are in your bed," I said. "The kind of family my mother was."

She looked at me then, her eyes so big and full I nearly choked on the tears, but I continued.

"My mother would never work jobs that kept her away from me, even when they would keep her warm and fed. I always thought I was ruining her life. But now I think she made the right choice. With me, she smiled and laughed. We had love between us. She didn't do that just for me, but for herself too. *She* needed that love. Everybody does."

"Oh, Bobby Lee," Nanette said, her voice quavering. Tears were streaming down her cheeks under the veil. I had meant to comfort her, and instead I had made her cry.

I mumbled an apology and made my awkward escape. As usual, I'd done the wrong thing. Maybe I just wasn't cut out for being good. In the grand foyer by the front door, I paused to consider. I had escaped the nuns, at least for the moment. This was my best chance to slip off into the city, to get a new start, but if I was going to do that, I needed money. I turned in the direction the men had gone.

I walked down a hall with flowered wallpaper until I came to the right door. I could feel the jazz music vibrating the doorknob. I stepped through into a haze of tobacco smoke and noise. Clovis and his boys were playing, while a group of Irish fiddlers looked on. I suppose they were taking turns. Beer, whiskey, and conversation were flowing. In the corner, a uniformed cop was raising a glass with Kelly and several other men, which brought my blood near to boiling. Still, I had come for one thing and one thing only. I spotted Alphonse Bujeau and Malcolm across the room near the band, and I made directly for them.

"Well, Bobby Lee, how are you liking Chicago?" Bujeau said, as if we were both just tourists who had encountered each other in the park.

"I like it fine, sir. But I'd enjoy it more if I had some money."

Bujeau threw his head back and laughed, as if I had just said the funniest thing in the world. "Did you hear that, Malcolm? He'd enjoy it more if he had money. Ain't that the way of the world, kid."

Malcolm smiled a little, as if his job required him to, then settled back into his usual expressionless silence.

I did not laugh or smile. "I'd like to collect what's owed me," I said. "One hundred eighty dollars."

"Look, kid, don't you know it's bad manners to talk business at a funeral?"

"I did what you asked and took a beating for it. I almost got killed by Kelly, and I told Hayworth exactly what you wanted. In fact, I even got the nuns to confirm the marriage, so Kelly can get his money and won't come after you. You owe me. You promised."

Bujeau glanced around for some other activity to distract him. "I'd love to take care of that now, but the thing is, kid, there was a horse running yesterday at the track. A real sure thing."

I narrowed my eyes at him. "If it was a sure thing, then you should have even *more* money."

"You'll have to wait until Nanette gets her settlement, same as everyone else. Now if you'll excuse me."

And with that, he pushed through the crowd away from me. Malcolm followed, but as he stepped past me, he paused. "Sorry, son, but you're never going to see that money. You should have demanded more up front. Or just stayed out of it." Then he walked away in Bujeau's wake.

He was right, of course. What a sap I'd been. I turned to go, only to run smack dab into Brian Kelly. I jumped back in alarm, but Kelly held his hands up to show he meant no harm.

"Relax, kid. It's your lucky day," he said with a predatory smile. "This is my boss, Mr. Dean O'Banion, and he wants to meet you. He runs the flower shop that did all the flowers for the funeral. Ain't they nice, Bobby Lee?"

I swallowed hard and agreed they were, though the words came out in an unintelligible squeak.

Mr. O'Banion smiled and offered a hand to shake. He had a soft, round face and green eyes that crinkled pleasantly at the corners. "A pleasure to meet you, Bobby," he said in a lilting Irish accent.

"You're a florist?" I said as I took his hand.

His grip was firm, almost painful. "I have a way with flowers." He put an arm around my shoulder and started walking me toward the corner by the door, where they had been when I first came in. "Mr. Kelly here has been telling me of his trip from New Orleans. He tells me you're looking for opportunities. Says you're green and brash, but you've got tenacity and style. Even pulled nuns and coppers into your racket, I understand. What would you say to a job, kid?"

This was exactly what I'd hoped for when I left New Orleans. In fact, it was more. I'd figured I'd have to start small and work my way up. But here I was, being offered a job by one of Chicago's top gangsters. And he thought I had style! There could be no better way to the top than being taken under the wing of the leader of the North Side Gang. Opportunity was knocking, and all I had to do was open the door. But somehow all I could hear was Sister Bridget, asking that question. *Is this the person you want to be, Bobby Lee?* And this time I knew the answer. I stepped back, gently removing O'Banion's arm from my shoulder.

"Thank you, sir, but I'm not sure I'll be staying in Chicago."

"Thinking of setting up on your own somewhere, kid? Think you can do better than Dean O'Banion?" Kelly growled.

"No, sir," I said. "I was thinking of going straight. I don't think I'm cut out for a life of crime."

Kelly laughed. "Likely story. You're an operator, kid, anyone can see that. You don't got it in you to go straight."

I shook my head. Brian Kelly had no idea what I had in me. Sure, he'd seen the lying and the sneaking, and maybe even the stealing I'd done. But I had more than that in me—a lot more. And it was better than he knew. Better, even, than I had known.

"Maybe you don't understand what I'm offering, kid." O'Banion said. "This can be a tough town for a kid like you who's got no one. I'm offering you more than just a job, you understand. I can take you under my wing. Be like a father to you, ain't that right, Kelly?"

"Sure, boss," Kelly said. "Just like a real family."

O'Banion turned back to me. "Come by Schofield's Flower Shop tomorrow and you can give me your answer then. Better yet, how about I send one of the boys around to collect you. You're at the Good Shepherd, I hear."

"There's really no need," I said.

"Anything for a good Catholic boy. I'll send someone by right around noon."

"I really have to go now," I said.

"Let me walk you to the door," Brian Kelly said. I tried to slip away into the crowd, but once again a firm arm clamped down over my shoulder. Side by side, Kelly and I moved through the sea of men, which parted for us as if Kelly were Moses. A murdering, thieving, gangster Moses.

"Maybe you don't understand the fine opportunity that's been offered here, kid," he said. "The exceptional honor Mr. O'Banion is doing you. To start out working directly for the boss, not working your way up through the dirtier side of the business."

"What I don't understand, Mr. Kelly, is what you and Mr. O'Banion are doing at the funeral of a man you killed! Putting on a show of sympathy for his whole family! You should be ashamed!" I knew my words were dangerous, but my restraint had snapped when Kelly had put his arm on my shoulder. I was tired of other people thinking I was theirs to lead around like a lost lamb.

Kelly gave me a scandalized look. "Of course we're here. It

would be a terrible insult for us not to pay our respects to a family that we have so long worked with. Poor Jimmy was one of our own, as was his father before him."

"But you killed him!"

Kelly gave a deep sigh, as if bracing himself to explain the obvious to a simpleton. "Jimmy's own carelessness killed him. Look at it this way. Say we were carpenters, building houses, and Jimmy had fallen off the roof. Would you expect us who worked with him not to pay our respects just because he'd died on the job?"

I glared at him. "Depends on whether or not you had loosened the shingles and given him a push."

Kelly gave a little laugh. "You got a tongue that will get you killed, kid. We've all got a weakness that'll be our undoing. For Jimmy, it was in taking on bad partners. It's a crying shame."

"And what about you, Mr. Kelly. What is your weakness?" I asked, looking at him through narrowed eyes. "What's going to get you killed? 'Cause I reckon what goes around comes around."

He gave me a cold smile, but I could see the specter of fear in his eyes too, the knowledge that maybe, just maybe, I was right—and that one day he'd be getting a push instead of giving it. I shook his arm from my shoulder and hightailed it down the hall and out of the house.

Once outside, I paused on the front steps. The city of Chicago stretched out before me. A fresh start. I could go wherever I wanted. I walked down the steps, turned left at the sidewalk, and made my way the few blocks to the church, just as I had promised.

Together, Sister Bridget and I caught a streetcar back to the House of the Good Shepherd. I was surprisingly content, except for one thing. I turned to Sister Bridget.

"Dean O'Banion said he was going to send someone after me at the House of the Good Shepard. He asked me to work for him, but I said no. I hope I haven't brought danger to y'all. I'd leave if it would be safer for you."

"Nonsense," the Sister said. "Dean O'Banion wouldn't dare defile a house of God with his violence. If he does, he'll have more than just God to contend with."

I didn't like the idea of bringing gangsters to the orphanage, but before I could protest any further, we found ourselves back at the House of the Good Shepard, with the good Sister ushering me inside and through to her office.

There she opened the door and stepped back to let me go in first. I admit, it should have made me suspicious, but I hadn't known nuns could be con artists too. Not until the door closed behind me and I saw I was alone inside, facing Sister Mary Magdalene herself, all the way from New Orleans. And from the look on her face, I suspected she'd left all of her charitable mercy behind.

HOUSE OF THE GOOD SHEPHERD, CHICAGO, ILLINOIS
4:07 P.M.

Sister Mary Magdalene. Ma'am. I didn't expect to see you," I said, my voice coming out in the same squeak I had given Dean O'Banion.

"I imagine not," she replied, her angular face registering no pleasure at all in our meeting. I doubted I looked all that overjoyed either. "You have caused a great deal of trouble, Robert Claremont. I hope you know that. A *great deal* of trouble."

"Yes, ma'am. I'm sorry. I will repay the poor box, I swear."

"Don't swear, Robert. Sit down." She moved to the chair behind the desk and lowered herself into it. This didn't bode well. We seemed to be settling in for a long talk. Reluctantly, I walked to the chair opposite her and sat.

"Explain to me, if you can, why you ran away, Robert," she said, her eyes burrowing into me.

I squirmed and looked away.

"I'm waiting," she said, in that tone that meant she wouldn't wait much longer.

"I wanted to get out on my own. To start over. Now that Maman is gone, there seemed no reason to stay in New Orleans."

"But all your friends are there. It's your home."

I shook my head. "I've got no friends."

"No friends? And what, exactly, am I? And Sister Bernadette? And all the others?"

"Um. Nuns?" I said, daring a glance at her face. Immediately I knew it hadn't been the right answer. Still, friends? I had never thought of them as my friends. Though they had fed me and cared for me, and stood by me at my mother's funeral. I lowered my eyes to the hands in my lap again.

"I'm sorry, Sister. I just wanted to be on my own, someplace new." Someplace where a reminder of my mother wasn't waiting around every corner. I didn't say this last part, but as usual, I didn't have to. Sister Mary Magdalene could read my every thought.

"You can't run away from the fact that she's dead, Robert." The words were so blunt that they knocked the wind out of me like a swift jab to the gut.

"Your mother will be with you no matter where you go, because she loved you."

I nodded again. "I know."

Her eyes were still hard upon me. I could feel them, like pins in a butterfly.

"Now I hear you want to be a criminal! I suppose you thought you'd steal from a poor box—from the hungry mouths of widows and orphans—to prove yourself? And these bruises—you've been fighting in a back alley, haven't you? And for what? All to prove yourself to those filthy gangsters terrorizing the good people of this city?"

"It's not like that! I wasn't planning to hurt anyone!" But even as I said it, I wasn't sure. Had it been like that? Could I have really ever believed that I could be a criminal and not hurt anyone? I knew better now, after my long two days with Nanette and her helpless baby.

Sister Mary Magdalene shook her head, her lips pursing in disgust. "I had thought more of you, Robert E. Lee Claremont. I had always thought, despite everything, that there was good in you. If your mother were alive, you would kill her all over again with this!"

"I *didn't* kill my mother!" I shouted, surprising the Sister so much her eyebrows nearly disappeared up into her wimple. Then the corner of her mouth gave a little twitch, fighting her granite complexion for a smile.

"I'm glad to hear you say that, Robert," she said, her tone mild.

"You are?"

"You've always been special to me because I've always known you were her angel of mercy. Not only did you save your mother's life, but more importantly, you saved her soul."

I stared at her, my mouth hanging open. *Special* to her? *Me?* Perhaps the long train ride had addled her brain.

"Your mother was a wild thing in her youth, a bit too free with the gentlemen. You know how those types of women end up. Forsaken by their families. Living on the street. Reaping the wages of sin."

"Maman wasn't like that!" I said. It was an accusation I had heard often enough as a kid without a father, and I had given more than one beating to kids who dared suggest it. I couldn't give a beating to the Sister, but my hands curled into fists all the same.

"No, she wasn't. Because she had you. From the moment

you were born, she changed her ways. I think you were the first person who loved her with a pure love. And she loved you back, with her whole heart and soul. You gave her joy and happiness, and a reason to live an honest, clean life. Yes, the Lord works in mysterious ways, and you are one of his most mysterious works of all." With that, that twitch at the corner of her mouth performed a miracle, turning stone to flesh, and she smiled a true, big smile—the kind that catches in the corners of the eyes and crinkles them up and makes them look like they're laughing. For a moment I thought she was going to reach out and tousle my hair. The sheer horror of the possibility nearly knocked me out of my chair.

Fortunately, she seemed to realize what was happening and got hold of herself. She cleared her throat and tipped up her chin, so she could look at me down the long length of her nose. "I have some business to attend to here in Chicago tomorrow. You will assist the good Sisters in the orphanage here, to keep out of trouble and to repay them for their hospitality. We will return home on the first train after my business is complete," she said, the crisp, stern tone right back into her voice where it belonged. I breathed a sigh of relief.

"Yes, ma'am," I said. Then I remembered what that business was, and the huge favor she was doing Nanette LeBlanc. In light of the new, softer Sister I'd seen, I couldn't help venturing a question. "How did you get the police to call Sergeant Hayworth home?" I asked.

"Fortunately for both of us, his captain is a moral man. He did not want an innocent woman to hang any more than you did."

"And what about the marriage record?" I asked.

She frowned. "Again, the Lord works in mysterious ways, Robert. That's all you ever need know. Now, I believe Sister Bridget needs your help in the nursery."

"Thank you, Sister," I said as I stood.

She nodded once and I turned to leave, thinking to myself that she wasn't such a bad old bird after all.

"And Robert," she said, stopping me in my tracks before I could reach the door.

"Yes, Sister?"

"Don't think any of this absolves you from paying back the poor box. We'll be discussing your full penance when we get back to New Orleans."

"Yes, Sister," I said, and slipped out the door, fairly certain that the payback was going to extend well beyond the handful of change I'd originally taken.

JUNE 1, 1923
CENTRAL STATION, CHICAGO, ILLINOIS
7:45 A.M.

Sister Mary Magdalene's business apparently took somewhat longer than she had expected, because I spent the next three days working from dawn to dusk in the House of the Good Shepherd. The Sisters had plenty for me to do, mostly in the bowels of the orphanage, boiling soiled diapers, scrubbing floors, peeling hundreds of pounds of potatoes before supper, and washing mountains of plates afterward.

On the evening of the third day, Sister Mary Magdalene announced we'd be on the 8:20 a.m. train for home the next day. As the sun rose, we were on a streetcar, bound for the station.

"I met your friend Nanette O'Halloran. She speaks very warmly of your kindness to her on the train," the Sister said as we rattled along.

"Did she get the insurance money?" I asked.

"Yes, I believe she did."

I let out a breath, feeling as if I'd been holding it for a long time. "That's a relief."

"She inquired about you. I told her we would be returning to New Orleans on the train today. She wishes you all the best."

I nodded, thanked her, and looked back out the window. I would miss Nanette, and the others—or at least some of them. My ticket north had not been wasted, even if I hadn't gotten what I came for. I had helped her get a good home and a family for herself and her child.

The train was already loading when we arrived on the platform, but before we found our car to board, a little streak charged across it toward me and grabbed me around the waist.

"Bobby Lee, you're back!" Terrance said excitedly, as he gave me a big squeeze. "Are you coming back to New Orleans with us?"

"Hi, Terrance," I said, peeling him off me and looking around. "I didn't think you'd still be in Chicago."

Terrance giggled. "We ain't still in Chicago, Bobby. We been back to New Orleans and back up here since we saw you last!"

"Oh, right," I said, smiling. "Where's Leon?"

"Wait till you see!" he said, and grabbing my free hand, he pulled me and the Sister through the crowd to the baggage car, where a whole crew of men were loading trunks and crates. There, in a new uniform, was Leon. He looked my way and flashed a smile, but didn't stop what he was doing.

"He got a real job?"

Terrance nodded, beaming with pride.

"But he isn't old enough," I said.

"Shh," Terrance said, but then couldn't resist adding, behind his hand but in a clear voice, "He fibbed."

"So if Leon's got a job, who's looking after you?" I asked.

"This is my granddaddy's last run. He's riding home in style, and me with him. He says that once we get back to New

Orleans, he and me are gonna stay home when my pop is cutting cotton. I'm gonna miss Leon, though."

Leon came near us to retrieve a trolley full of luggage. "You won't have time to miss me," he said. "You'll be going to school."

"What about you?" I asked.

Leon shrugged. "My momma schooled me enough before she died," he said.

It didn't seem quite fair to me, but as I watched the muscles strain across his shoulders and back as he pushed the trolley, I saw something else too. I saw his pride in doing a good, honest job to take care of his family. Leon would be all right.

"What an enterprising young man," Sister Mary Magdalene said, apparently observing the same. "You could learn a thing or two from him, Robert."

"Yes, ma'am," I said. "I think I already have."

"How come you're going back to New Orleans? Didn't things work out in Chicago?" Terrance asked, eyeing Sister Mary Magdalene with suspicion.

"No. Not so good."

"Maybe you could come live with us now that Granddaddy's staying," Terrance said.

"I don't think so, Terrance. But thank you."

Terrance looked momentarily crestfallen, but then another thought perked him up. "But we can sit with you on the train, right? Least till we gets to Kentucky."

I glanced up at Sister Mary Magdalene and she nodded. "That would be mighty fine, Terrance," I agreed.

"It looks like someone else has come to say goodbye," the Sister said, pointing.

I looked where she indicated to see Malcolm approaching, accompanied by a woman in a burgundy dress and hat, carrying a baby. It took me a few seconds to realize it was Nanette, no longer dressed and veiled in widow's weeds. I glanced around, nervous about whoever might be with them, but I saw no one. Nanette smiled at me. I relaxed and smiled back.

"Bobby Lee, I'm glad we caught you. The Sister said you'd be returning this morning." She pressed a cookie tin into my hands. "For your journey."

"Thanks. I guess everything has worked out for you?"

She nodded, looking grave. "The money came through, though most of it went to O'Banion to pay off the debt at the Cajun Queen. That ends Jimmy's involvement with the North Siders." A ghost of pain passed across her face at the mention of Jimmy, as I figured it would for a while. Things working out now didn't change the fact that he was dead. Nanette drew in a deep breath before she spoke again. "And I signed over my interest in the club to Alphonse. Clovis thought maybe I should keep it, but there are too many memories there." The look of pain came back, pulling at my own heartstrings. I knew exactly what she meant.

"Anyway," she continued, "knowing Alphonse, he will entangle the place in debt again in no time. And I sure don't need to be involved in that." Now she smiled, and I could see it was a smile of relief. She was more beautiful than ever.

"That's good," I said, then felt embarrassed for no reason at all. So I added, "I wish you the best."

She blushed and fidgeted with the baby's blanket. "The thing is, I've thought about what you said at the funeral. About love and family. You must have come from a very special family to understand that."

I shook my head. "No, ma'am. I never had a family. But my mother loved me very much. And I've always had the Sisters."

Nanette nodded. "I never had a family either, not until I joined up with Clovis and his boys. They were like a family to me, but I didn't rightly understand that. I thought my baby needed a bona fide family—one that shared his blood.

"But these folks in Chicago, their home is so . . . so cold, I guess. My son will have a proper family here, but not proper love. And that's what I figure most makes a house a home, just like you said."

"I'm sure they must love Jimmy's son, in their own way," I said, but my talent for telling good lies must have slipped away with my newfound goodness.

She shook her head. "I'm leaving Chicago with the Clovis Dupré Orchestra, Bobby Lee. Like I said, they've been my family all along, I was just too blind to see it. We won't have a big house or a lot of money. But I don't think we need that to have a home."

I glanced at Sister Mary Magdalene, expecting her to condemn Nanette's decision, but if she had such thoughts, she was keeping them locked behind an unreadable expression.

"I don't think so either," I said. I looked at Malcolm, who still stood silently behind her. "Are you headed back to the Cajun Queen?"

"Nope."

"Malcolm no longer works for Mr. Bujeau," Nanette said.

"He went too far, hurting you and Miss Nanette," Malcolm

said. "I'm going with Miss Nettie and the orchestra. Someone needs to take care of the baby while she's onstage, and I'm tired of having to bully folks."

I almost laughed at the thought of big Malcolm playing nursemaid to the tiny baby, but then I remembered the tender look that had come over him when he had spoken to me of Nanette before, and I realized that just like me, there was more to him as well.

Nanette glanced at the Sister. "We came to meet you because we thought you might like to come with us, Bobby Lee. We're headed for Cleveland in an hour, then on east and eventually to New York. Clovis could use another hand hauling instruments and equipment. He's offering you the job, but it's more than a job, really. Like I said, Clovis and the boys are a family."

"That's not a real family. And it's certainly not a home," Sister Mary Magdalene said, pulling me a step toward the train.

"Home is where the heart is, Sister," I replied. "Isn't that what the Bible says?"

"I don't think the Bible says any such thing," she said, giving me that look that said *Why don't you pay attention to what I teach you?*

"The orchestra lives on the road a good deal of the time. So, it wouldn't be a home in the traditional sense," Nanette admitted. "And we aren't a true family in the eyes of the law, what with some folks being colored and some not. Some people might call that wrong."

"We are all God's children," the Sister said stiffly.

"But he'd be loved and cared for, and want for nothing. I promise you that."

"I'd love to come with you," I said, getting ready to make

my apology. There was no way the Sisters of Charitable Mercy would release me from my penance to go live the sinful life of traveling musicians.

Then a miracle happened. Sister Mary Magdalene's grip on my hand loosened, then released.

"The decision is yours, Bobby Lee," she said. "You'll be fourteen in a few months, so you are old enough to decide."

I drew in a deep breath. There was no decision to be made. "Thank you, Sister!"

"Then you won't be riding the train with us?" Terrance asked, his little face puckering up in dismay. I admit, it gave a firm tug on my heartstrings.

"I'm afraid not, Terrance. I'm going with Nanette and Malcolm. But you're going home with your granddaddy."

"And I get to go to school. But I'm gonna miss you, Bobby Lee."

"Tell you what," I said, squatting down, eye to eye with him. "How about I send you a postcard when I get where I'm going?"

"Where are you going?" Terrance asked.

I shrugged. "All over, I guess."

"I'd like to get a postcard from all over," he admitted.

So Nanette dug a pencil and paper out of her pocketbook, and we wrote down an address that Leon carefully dictated to us. It cheered up Terrance, and I admit, I liked the idea of keeping up a correspondence. After all, Terrance and Leon were the first real friends I'd ever had.

"You'll write me back too, won't you?" I asked.

"Soon as I learn to write," he promised. Then he looked forlornly at the cookie tin in my hands.

"I s'pose if you ain't coming with us, we don't get cookies?" he said.

I laughed and gave him the tin. After all, I was going off with Nanette and Clovis and little Jimmy Jr. Somehow, I figured there'd be plenty of sweetness to go around, even without the cookies.

With that, I turned to the Sister. "I'm sorry I can't pay back the poor box just yet."

"Oh, don't worry about that," she said.

I stared, wondering what had come over her.

Her eyebrows arched up in reply. "I met your friend Dean O'Banion when he came looking for you at the House of the Good Shepherd."

My stomach knotted at the mention of the name. I had forgotten all about his promise. "He came looking for me?"

"I had a little chat with him, and through the grace of God he found it in his heart to make a sizable contribution to the Sisters of Charitable Mercy and the House of the Good Shepherd. Such nice Catholic boys, those Irish."

I admit, my mouth was hanging open. I'd thought I'd have to go all the way to Chicago to learn the art of the scam, when I'd been living with a master all this time.

"Are you sure it was the grace of God, Sister?"

"I will say this one last time, Robert: the Lord works in mysterious ways." And with that, she pulled me into a tight embrace. "Just remember, there will always be a home for you with the Sisters of Charitable Mercy, should you need it. I will pray that you won't."

I nodded, feeling surprisingly choked up. "I will write," I said. "I promise."

"Don't worry about Bobby Lee, Sister," Nanette said. "He's been my guardian angel since we left New Orleans. Now I'll be his."

Sister Mary Magdalene smiled and patted the beat-up suitcase she carried, which I now realized also carried O'Banion's contribution. "That's our Robert E. Lee Claremont. A guardian angel," she said.

The whistle blew and the conductor called out his final warning from the train. Sister Mary Magdalene sprang into action, herding Terrance aboard as if he was her charge. I turned to Nanette and Malcolm.

"Cleveland?" I said.

"Cleveland," Nanette replied, threading her arm though mine and turning back toward the main terminal. "Platform 17. Clovis and his boys are waiting for us. Tell me, Bobby Lee. Have you ever considered playing the piano? I could teach you. I'll be teaching Malcolm too."

I smiled as I walked. To think I had believed I would never have a home again. This wasn't anything like I had expected it to be. This was much better.

AUTHOR'S NOTE

In 1970, Steve Goodman immortalized the Illinois Central's passenger train that ran between Chicago and New Orleans with his song "City of New Orleans," a tune that has repeatedly climbed the charts in the performances of Arlo Guthrie, Willie Nelson, and Johnny Cash. While the train they call the City of New Orleans did not make her debut on the line until 1947, the Illinois Central Railroad between New Orleans and Chicago dates back to 1856, when it was the longest rail line in the world. Over the decades, it carried hundreds of thousands of people and millions of dollars' worth of freight through the heartland of America. In the early decades of the twentieth century, it was a major avenue of the "Great Migration" as African Americans moved north to industrial cities like Chicago, pulled by the promise of jobs and pushed by the injustice of segregation under Jim Crow laws.

New Orleans was hit hard by the relatively late adoption of Jim Crow laws. The city had a long history of intermixing, dating back to its French origins. Significant segregation began only after 1890, when Louisiana passed its first Jim Crow law, a full ten to twenty years after most other Southern states. The 1890 law called for segregation on railcars, and the challenge that the New Orleans black community put forward to that law was one of the most famous, and disastrous, landmarks of civil rights history. Homer Plessy, a French-speaking Creole who was one-eighth black, or "octoroon" in the language of the era, deliberately "passed" as a white man and rode in a white railcar, setting up his prearranged arrest. The plan was to show the arbitrary nature of the law of the land (a man who looked white and was seven-eighths white being categorized as "black") and to pose a legal challenge to segregation. However, when, in 1896, the United States Supreme Court upheld "separate but equal" in *Plessy v. Ferguson*, Jim Crow laws were given a green light to flourish throughout the South. The verdict was not overturned until 1967, three years after the Civil Rights Act of 1964 made segregation illegal throughout America.

In New Orleans, segregation meant the members of a long-established, middle-class Creole community, many of them educated in first-rate white schools and colleges, suddenly found themselves redefined as black and categorized with the poorer African-American community. The face of the city, and its music, were changed dramatically. Many historians see this as a pivotal element in the birth of jazz, as classically trained Creole musicians intermingled with African American folk musicians.

While the South was pulling itself apart along color lines, Chicago was struggling with increased ethnic tension over Prohibition and the control of illegal alcohol. In the early 1920s, Al Capone was not the only powerful mobster making the streets of the city dangerous. Dean O'Banion, an unimposing florist and ruthless leader of the primarily Irish American North Side Gang, was battling the Italian American Johnny Torrio and Al Capone for supremacy in the bootleg business. O'Banion's murder by his rivals in 1924 (the flowers at the funeral were reportedly spectacular!) sparked the bloody gang war that culminated in the infamous Valentine's Day Massacre of 1929. (This might appease any readers who felt Kelly and O'Banion didn't quite get their comeuppance in my story set in 1923.)

By now, perhaps you will see many of the threads of history I have tried to pull together in my story. Drawing inspiration from Homer Plessy's courageous act of civil disobedience, I have attempted to show the senseless and arbitrary nature of race law in early twentieth-century America, and the hardships it created for the people of New Orleans, most especially its African-American and mixed-race populations. And like Homer Plessy, I have chosen to do it by putting an octoroon on a segregated train, a setting which allowed me to explore the way the rules—and even the definition of who was white—changed on a twenty-three-hour journey north.

To flesh out the details of that journey, I used an original, early twentieth-century timetable to create the stops and times in each chapter, and a variety of historic photographs, postcards, and oral histories to accurately re-create those stops and the activities that occurred at them. One of the most wonderful resources I found was the website Fulton KY's Historic African American Railroaders, filled with images and oral histories of African Americans who worked for the Illinois Central Railroad, at http://fultonkysafricanamericanrailroaders.weebly.com/railroad-man.html.

I also relied on the Internet and a few French Canadian friends to help me with the expressions and the spelling differences of Cajun French, a dialect descended from the Acadian French of Canada.

But for me, this story all started with Steve Goodman's "City of New Orleans." The idea came to me in the shower one morning (yes, I sing in the shower), after the song had been stuck in my head for about a week. I thought about the lovely images of ordinary people contained within it, and wondered what the backstory of those people might be. And so, if you read my story carefully, you will see my nods to many of the details Mr. Goodman recorded on his southbound odyssey, scattered throughout my northbound story set fifty years earlier.

ACKNOWLEDGMENTS

I wish to express my gratitude for the many people who helped make this book happen. I received helpful feedback from critique partners and readers, including Jennifer J. Stewart, Ann Bedichek Braden, Mike Hassel, Kiersten Stevenson, Heather Alexander, and Dhonielle Clayton. I had useful conversations about Acadian French with Kat Kruger and Hélène Boudreau. I enjoyed ongoing writerly support and encouragement from my lovely friends of Write-o-rama, Erin Murphy's Dog, and my beloved community of writers in Colorado—you know who you are! And finally, a huge thank-you to my profoundly insightful editor, Kelly Loughman (you're totally forgiven regarding the coffin scene), the skillful artist Oriol Vidal who created the cover, Jennifer Thermes, who drew the map (I've always wanted a book with a map inside it!), and all the fine people at Holiday House who turned my pile of pages into this beautiful book.